"What? *I don't*

Sarah-Jane struggled to bring her voice down to its normal register. "I don't even have a boyfriend. I told you that already!"

"Then what *are* you hiding? If you weren't interested in seeing me again, you could have just said so." Wyatt's lips tilted almost charmingly, except he didn't look at all amused. "I wouldn't have liked it, but I'm a grown man. I would have accepted it and left you alone."

"I don't want you to leave me alone," she said faintly.

He'd exhaled as if he'd actually thought for a second she'd have felt otherwise, and covered her hand with his. "Then, tell me, Savannah. Why do I have the strong sense that you're trying to avoid me?"

Just tell him. The words seemed to scream through her head. "I've been lying to you." She pushed out the words.

His hand didn't move on hers, but she felt his stillness. "About what?"

She felt her shoulders bowing forward and made herself sit up straighter. "About everything."

Dear Reader,

Welcome back to Red Rock and another Fortune Family adventure! Last time we were together, one of the Atlanta branch of the family was planning her wedding. Now, here we are again, at the reception of that very wedding, where five very handsome Fortune men are celebrating. They're entirely sure that they won't succumb to the Red Rock matrimonial habit, but there are five very intriguing women who just might change their minds.

This is exactly what Wyatt Fortune learns when he meets Sarah-Jane Early, who turns out to be so much more than he'd ever expected.

It's always such a pleasure to be able to glance in on the Fortune families I've come to know and love, and fall all over again for the newcomers. Equally pleasurable for me is having an opportunity to work with not only the talented authors who are revisiting the series, but having the chance to work with the talented new authors who join the fold along the way!

I hope you'll find this new trip back to Red Rock with the Atlanta Fortunes just as much fun as I did.

Allison Leigh

HER
NEW YEAR'S
FORTUNE

ALLISON LEIGH

HARLEQUIN®

entertain, enrich, inspire™

Special thanks and acknowledgment
to Allison Leigh for her contribution
to the Fortunes of Texas: Southern Invasion continuity.

Recycling programs
for this product may
not exist in your area.

ISBN-13: 978-0-373-65715-5

HER NEW YEAR'S FORTUNE

www.Harlequin.com

Printed in U.S.A.

ALLISON LEIGH

There is a saying that you can never be too rich or too thin. Allison doesn't believe that, but she does believe that you can *never* have enough books! When her stories find a way into the hearts—and bookshelves—of others, Allison says she feels she's done something right. Making her home in Arizona with her husband, she enjoys hearing from her readers at Allison@allisonleigh.com or P.O. Box 40772, Mesa, AZ 85274-0772.

For Greg, for making me see the wings.

Chapter One

New Year's Eve. A night of mystery.

Just like *she* was mysterious. Beautiful. Exotic. And definitely mysterious.

Dark, auburn hair spilled in waves down her back, kissing the golden spine revealed by the cut-down-to-there black cocktail dress that clung to her lithe figure. Her companion's dark blue gaze was focused intently on her face…dropping to her lips as she took a small sip of her martini. Slightly dirty, just the way she'd ordered. She lowered the cocktail and leaned a little closer to him, feeling more than slightly naughty. Beneath the table, she slipped her foot out of her sinfully high black heels and subtly slid her toes along his ankle…

"Excuse me, miss. Miss? *Miss?*"

The fantasy spinning inside Sarah-Jane Early's head popped like a bubble of spent soap and she focused on the tuxedo-clad man standing in front of the hostess station she was manning at Red, looking none too patient. She was there not to daydream, but to help see to the needs of every guest of the wedding reception that had commandeered the popular Mexican restaurant for the night, and she quickly smiled. "Yes, sir, how can I help you?"

The man tugged at his skewed bow tie, casting a glance off to one side. "How do I get to the Red Rock Inn?" His question was hurried, and muttered half under his breath. She could have told him he needn't have bothered trying to be so quiet. For the past three hours, the music from the reception had made conversations nearly impossible. She leaned a little closer to give him the directions to the hotel. He nodded, and took time to thank her before moving away to hold out his hand to the woman he'd obviously been waiting for.

In seconds, they were hurrying out the front door of the restaurant, the man's arm wrapped possessively around the woman's hips. It was obvious to anyone with eyes in their head that the couple couldn't wait to be alone.

She knew there was no point in envying a couple in love… or even a couple in lust, or she'd be spending her life in a constant state of envy. Still, Sarah-Jane sighed and shifted her weight from one foot to the other.

Fantasizing about wearing killer heels was one thing. Actually doing it was another. She wished she'd have just worn a pair of shoes from her own closet. She had a pair of black pumps. Admittedly they were nearly ten years old, purchased by her mother who had insisted that Sarah-Jane needed to wear the modestly-heeled things for her high school graduation. But they were leather and having been worn only a few times since, were still in good condition.

She glanced down at the shoes she was currently wearing. If she were honest, the only thing in common *these* shoes had with the old ones in her closet were that they were black. She twisted one foot this way and that, and sighed again, a little wistfully. The shoes that Maria Mendoza had insisted she wear *were* beautiful. The velvety suede was as black as midnight and certainly suited the clinging black cocktail dress she was wearing better than her sensible old pumps.

Just thinking about the dress had Sarah-Jane's fingertips twitching at the hem of it, as if she could eke out another few inches of cloth where there was none. The hem of the dress stayed midway down her thighs, where it had been since she'd donned the garment earlier that day. She couldn't do anything about the hem anymore than she could do something about the diagonally-slashed cutout neckline that exposed much more of Sarah-Jane's cleavage than she liked. If she weren't positively devoted to Maria, who not only owned the restaurant along with her husband but also owned the knitting shop where Sarah-Jane *really* worked as an assistant manager, there's no way she'd have worn something so unsuitable out in public. She was a lot more comfortable in the pullover shirts and khaki pants that she wore at The Stocking Stitch. She wouldn't win any fashion awards, but at least she didn't have to worry that people might think she believed she could carry off such a look.

Her gaze drifted from the empty lobby area of the restaurant back toward the bar where many of the wedding guests had migrated. Most of the wedding party remained, though Emily Fortune and her brand-new husband, Max Allen, had already departed. As had many of the older guests, leaving the younger crowd to stay on and party into the night.

There wasn't an unsuitably-clad person in the bunch.

What else would one expect when the bride was part of the wealthy Fortune family? To a one, every single person who'd entered the restaurant that evening had looked like they'd stepped out of the pages of a fashion magazine.

Her fingertips searched for her hem and tugged.

"Sarah-Jane."

The sound of her name had her quickly straightening and

she turned to find Marcos Mendoza gesturing from near the kitchen. He managed Red, but was also married to a Fortune of his own, and since that Fortune happened to be the little sister of the bride, he'd also been part of the wedding party. She left her post at the hostess station and hurried toward him. "Yes?"

"I think it's safe for you to clear out," he offered. "There's still a little New Year's Eve left for you to enjoy."

She kept her smile in place. "I arranged to be here the entire evening, Marcos." She certainly didn't have anything more exciting waiting for her at home. Her roommate, Felicity, was at a party, and there had never been any handsome men in Sarah-Jane's life who were anxious to ring in anything with her, much less a new year. At least by helping out Maria, she was doing something productive. "I know Maria wanted all of you to be able to enjoy the wedding as guests rather than staff. I can still help out in the kitchen or something."

He smiled wryly. "Well, I'm not about to turn down willing help. But you'd be a waste in the kitchen dressed like you are." Off duty and wedding guest or not, he was still clearly in management mode. He quickly scanned the restaurant, then nodded with decision. "Cindy's slammed at the bar; if you don't mind grabbing a tray and starting to collect the empties—"

"I don't mind," she assured, and was glad to head that way. Being busy was always preferable to standing around letting her wandering mind conjure up silly fantasies of a faceless man who had eyes only for her.

Ignoring her aching feet, she headed toward the bar, crossing between the crowded tables. She would have had to have been blind not to notice the line of men bellied up to the bar as she rounded it, but she kept her gaze focused on the new task at hand. Cindy, the temporary bartender that Maria had hired for the evening, did look slammed, barely glancing at

Sarah-Jane when she found the trays behind the bar. She retrieved one and quickly turned back around, heading to the tables once more. In minutes, she'd filled the tray with abandoned glasses, and she aimed toward the swinging door leading to the kitchen. She had to pass by the line of men at the bar again on the way, and as she did, one of them stuck out his arm behind him.

"Here you go, hon." Even above the music, his voice was deep and filled with a Southern drawl. The man didn't glance at her, and she automatically took the glass, looking away shyly when her gaze collided with the dark blond-haired man sitting next to him. "Wyatt, what the hell do you mean you're not coming back to Atlanta?" she heard him demand.

Not wanting to appear to be eavesdropping, she stacked the glass precariously inside another, and aimed for the kitchen again. The tray was too heavy to carry one handed, and she turned, using her hip to push through the swinging door.

Her gaze couldn't help glancing toward the men at the bar. She'd been the one to seat them at their assigned tables when they'd arrived, so she knew they were all related to the bride, though she wasn't sure exactly how. There were five of them, all wearing similar black suits that looked as if they'd been born to them. And each one was better looking than the last. They'd arrived without women on their arms, but Sarah-Jane had a hard time believing that they'd all be leaving without one.

At least she'd have plenty of details to give Felicity in the morning.

As if he'd felt her attention, the blond-haired man at the end of the bar sitting next to the glass-giver looked her way. He'd pulled his silver tie loose around his throat and looked like he couldn't wait to get out of it altogether.

Her breath stopped up in her chest and the door that she'd

just nudged open swung back again, bumping her square on her rump. She jumped, feeling her cheeks flush.

But the man who'd seemed to be staring right into her eyes merely lifted the shot glass he was holding and tossed back the amber contents, his focus turning again to his companions.

He hadn't noticed her at all.

Feeling foolish, she backed through the swinging door and dumped off the empties with the kid manning the dishwasher. What was she thinking? Men like that didn't give women like Sarah-Jane a second glance. Not a serious one, anyway.

Never had. Never would.

With that reminder firmly in her head, she took her empty tray and went out to fill it again.

"I mean there's been a change of plans," Wyatt repeated patiently, while his cousin Michael eyed him with clear impatience. "We're staying here in Red Rock." Wyatt looked past his cousin to his three brothers. First Asher, then Shane, then Sawyer. Willing them to nod. Back him up. They'd already made the decision, and just because his brothers had been drinking steadily since they'd hit the bar didn't mean anything had changed.

Not back in Atlanta, that was for damn sure.

Asher finally nodded. Sawyer did, too. Shane's nod was a little slower in coming. "That's what we said," he muttered, though he didn't look any too happy about it.

Wyatt loved his brothers. But if anyone was going to side with their father, it was going to be Shane.

As if he'd heard Wyatt's thoughts, his brother shot him a look, then gestured toward the pretty bartender with his glass. Without a word, the lanky blonde tipped the bottle of whiskey, pouring out another shot before she turned and filled several margarita glasses for a waiting cocktail waitress.

"You're telling me you've all just up and decided to take

unscheduled vacations from JMF Financial?" Michael was still shaking his head, disbelief thinning his lips. "A month ago you were complaining because you didn't know how to fit in a week to come out here for Emily's wedding."

A month ago—hell, even less than that—Wyatt and his brothers had still had a rug firmly under their boots.

Thanks to their father, now they didn't.

"It's more than a vacation." His voice was flat. "We're not going back. Period."

Michael frowned, but he was obviously just as confused by the pronouncement as he was annoyed at the change of plans. His cousin didn't like being left out of the loop, but Wyatt didn't feel like explaining the reasons behind their decision. Not here at Emily's wedding reception, anyway, where the loud music was making any kind of conversation more public than he liked.

"What'd you all decide to do? Hang around Red Rock and find yourselves wives?" Michael's voice was heavy with sarcasm. "That's what everyone else in this family who sticks around in Red Rock for more than a few days seems to do. Puts their heads right into a marital noose."

"Hell no!" Sawyer visibly shuddered. He was twenty-seven—two years younger than Wyatt—and the idea of marriage was clearly as far from his mind as it was Wyatt's. Shane was nodding, too. And Asher...well, Asher had already gone through one divorce. He just stared into his drink and said nothing.

"Then what the *hell's* going on?"

Wyatt's jaw was so tight, it ached. He looked away from his cousin's confounded face and his brothers' stoic ones. The hostess who'd seated them was still moving around the tables, loading up her little round tray with empty glasses. He watched the sway of her shapely backside as she disappeared through the swinging kitchen door with her latest load.

She looked about average height—shorter than the tall bartender—and from the gleaming auburn hair that she'd tied back in a knot to the high-heeled shoes she was wearing, she looked anything but average.

Watching her throughout the evening had at least provided a nice diversion when he'd felt his mood turning black.

"Maybe we need to go back to Atlanta," Shane suggested. "Shutting that door *is* pretty damn permanent, Wy. Even you've got to admit that."

Wyatt eyed his older brother. The eldest of his brothers at thirty-two, Shane was chief operating officer of JMF Financial. Slightly higher up the food chain than Wyatt was, but neither Wyatt's nor Sawyer's or Asher's stake in the future of the company was any less important. "We can discuss it later."

"But—"

"He's right," Asher said quietly. He was only a year younger than Shane, and as was often the case, when he *did* speak up, he was the voice of reason. "This isn't the place."

"You've all lost your minds," Michael muttered. He was older than them all, and cousins or not, was used to calling the shots. "What*ever* is going on. You're just gonna up and leave everything you've worked for at JMF. To stay in Red Rock." He shook his head at what he clearly considered unfathomable, but thankfully dropped the subject and waved his finger over his squat glass. The bartender saw the signal, and poured him yet another shot.

The blonde was good at her job. Efficient. Didn't linger, listening in. The reception had an open bar, but Wyatt figured he'd still leave the girl a healthy tip. She'd certainly earned it.

The voluptuous hostess slipped past again and Wyatt tracked her progress without really realizing it. The bartender was a pretty blonde who looked like she'd be just as at home batting around a volleyball on the beach as she did working behind the busy bar. In contrast, the hostess was a stunning knockout with enough curves to please a Formula 1 driver.

Wyatt wasn't a race car driver. And while he usually tended toward tall, athletic women more like the bartender, he found himself definitely appreciating the hostess's heady curves. Watching her was a lot more pleasurable than dwelling on the mess they'd left behind in Atlanta.

A mess that he and his brothers had had no hand in creating, but one they sure as hell had to live with.

The bartender stopped in front of him. "Sure I can't get you something stronger, Mr. Fortune?"

He shook his head. He'd learned a long time ago that he couldn't keep up with his brothers when it came to liquor. "I'll stick with the soda, thanks."

"Designated driver?"

"On occasion." At this stage, neither his brothers nor his cousin looked like they were going to stop drinking anytime soon, so maybe he would be filling that role that night, as well. Michael had arrived at the reception with the wedding party in one of the limousines. Wyatt and his brothers had driven over in one of their rental cars.

"Let me know if I can get you anything else," the bartender offered, and experience told Wyatt she wasn't only talking about drinks. But even after conveying the message, she was already in motion again. Wyatt turned against the bar until it was behind his back and leaned on his elbows. He wasn't interested in the bartender. He wasn't interested in anyone.

From the corner of his eye, he caught a glimpse of auburn hair and his gaze followed it.

"Hard to believe Emily's married," Michael mused, beside him.

Wyatt grunted in agreement. His died-in-the-wool career cousin had been as devoted to FortuneSouth Enterprises as her brother, Michael, still was. Like Wyatt and his brothers, his cousins had been raised up in their father's Atlanta-based business, though FortuneSouth was a telecommunications company while Wyatt's father, James Marshall Fortune, had founded the financial firm, JMF. Everyone in the family knew there was no love lost between James and his younger brother, John, even though only a few years separated them. James hadn't even bothered coming to Red Rock for his niece's wedding.

But everyone also knew that the two brothers were pretty much cut from the same cloth—workaholics who were driven to succeed, and had. Many times over.

John, however, had never pulled a stunt like Wyatt's father, James, had. Not as far as he was aware, at least. Emily had quit working for her father because she'd followed in the footsteps of all of her siblings—save Michael—who'd transplanted themselves to Red Rock, all in the name of love.

"The Red Rock curse," Michael murmured beside him, his thoughts obviously running the same course as Wyatt's. "Weddings every time we turn around. Enough to give a man the willies."

"Weddings aren't always a curse," Asher countered.

Michael's eyebrows shot up. "*How* long ago did you sign those divorce papers of yours?"

Asher's lips thinned. "Some marriages work."

"Read the statistics. These days, more of 'em don't," Michael returned. "You won't find me ever going down on bended knee." He had to raise his voice over the pulsing beat of the music. He turned until his back was to the bar like Wyatt's and sipped his drink. "Not that I'm against women, mind you," he added, his gaze on the gaggle of young women who'd crowded on to the dance floor. They obviously didn't care that none of their dates were out there with them; they were dancing and shaking, shoes kicked off and hooting as if they didn't have a care in the world.

Wyatt's gaze moved on from them and he realized he was searching for a sign of the hostess again. She was probably about the age of the women on the dance floor. It was too bad she was working and wasn't out there, too. But he didn't spot her. Maybe she'd already gotten off duty and had left.

He thought about leaving himself, but controlled the urge and eventually, the reception finally started to wind down. Wyatt had counted off several more rounds of drinks that his brothers and Michael knocked back, and they started making noises about checking out what was left of the New Year's Eve festivities elsewhere in town. Particularly the prospect of encountering some unattached lovelies.

Wyatt wasn't interested in more music or booze or women. He was interested in the truth behind his father's inexplicable betrayal. A truth that, so far, hadn't been forthcoming from any quarter, least of all the old man.

"Last call, gentlemen." Despite working her tail off for several hours, the bartender looked as perky as ever. "Anything I can get you?"

"We're heading out, hon," Michael told her, his trademark smile in place. He reached over the bar for a clean glass and set it on the bar, then tucked several bills from his wallet into it. "You be sure and find some lucky man to kiss at midnight."

The bartender shook her head, looking rueful. "*Hon,* midnight came and went an hour ago."

Wyatt hid a smile, but typically, Michael let that little detail roll right off his back. "Every night has a midnight," he drawled.

"That it does," she agreed, her amusement deepening. She nudged the glass back toward Michael. "And that's not necessary tonight, Mr. Fortune." Her gaze took in the rest of them. "You boys going to be taking a cab, or is Mr. Designated Driver on duty?"

"They're cabbin' it," Wyatt answered before anyone else

could. The hostess had just reappeared through the kitchen door and his interest in getting out of there dwindled. He looked over at the bartender and swirled his glass in a circle on the bar. "Hit me one more time, would you please?"

"You bet." In seconds, she'd given him a fresh smile and a fresh soda before turning away to fill the flurry of orders she'd gotten for last call.

"Going to hang here for a while, huh?" Michael gave him a speculative look, hanging back while Wyatt's brothers headed to the front of the restaurant. Asher stopped for a moment to talk to the curvaceous hostess and Wyatt figured he was asking about arranging for a cab.

Again, his gaze held on the line of her creamy spine, revealed here and there by the intriguing cut-outs of her form-fitting black dress. "Gonna be quieter here than it will be wherever you guys decide to go," he told his cousin.

Michael laughed beneath his breath. "I've seen what you've been eyeing all night. *Quiet* isn't on your mind."

Wyatt's fingers tightened around the cold glass. It was easier to let his cousin think his distraction with the shapely hostess was responsible for his decision to hang back than to explain the black hole that was yawning open inside of him. After the last few days of wedding festivities, he just wanted to be left alone. "She's not a what, Mike." Nobody ever shortened Michael's name. "She's a who."

Michael's smile sharpened even more. "As long as whoever she is manages to help you lighten up, without you ending up down on *your* knee."

Wyatt grimaced. His cousin should know better. Marriage was no higher on Wyatt's list than it was on Michael's.

"Maybe you'll come to your senses about returning to Atlanta along the way," Michael finished. He reached across the bar and set the glass with the hefty tip he'd left on the bartender's stainless steel work area then gave Wyatt a slap on the shoulder before crossing the restaurant.

Despite the alcohol Wyatt knew he'd consumed, his cousin's steps were as sure as ever.

He exhaled and watched them all push through the front door of the restaurant. There was no way Wyatt would be reconsidering his decision about returning to Atlanta. He'd drawn the line in the sand. His father had stubbornly refused to explain his actions regarding the family company, JMF Financial. Which meant that, if anything, Wyatt would only be digging that line deeper and wider. He had right on his side, while his dad was drowning in wrong. There was just no other way to categorize James's decision to sell the company out from under them.

He slowly finished his drink, his thoughts turned inward and only when the D.J. finally stopped the music did he add his own contribution to the bartender's tip glass. She gave him a good-natured smile tinged with a hint of regret.

He pretended not to notice. He just wasn't interested. So he left the bar and the restaurant behind, and headed out into the cold night. He didn't have to bother saying his goodbyes to anyone in the family; they'd all left and he'd be seeing them again later in the morning at the brunch being held at their hotel. His mother had reminded him three separate times about the brunch, as if she'd suspected—correctly enough—that he'd had more than his fill of wedding folderol.

His rental car was only one of a few still remaining in the parking lot. When he reached it, he unlocked the car and climbed in. But instead of starting the engine, he sighed again, staring blindly at the steering wheel.

They hadn't broken the news to Clara yet that they wouldn't be going home. It didn't take a genius to know that his mother wouldn't be thrilled. She'd never been involved in the running of JMF, but she'd always been involved in her children.

The fact that they were all adults with their own lives hadn't changed that at all.

He raked back his hair, digging his fingers into the back of his tight neck. Deciding to draw that line in the sand had been the only thing to do, considering what their father had done. But how were they going to break the news to their mother? As far as she knew, they were all scheduled to leave for Atlanta after the brunch. They needed to let her know they wouldn't be accompanying her.

"Sir? Would you like a cab after all?"

Jerked from his thoughts, Wyatt frowned and looked up.

The hostess from the restaurant stood beside the car, a brilliant red scarf draped around her shoulders. She was leaning down slightly and even though the only light to speak of came from the dome light in the rental car, he could see the way her eyebrows crinkled together over her eyes. He was hard-pressed to know where to look—at those dark eyes of hers or the spectacular cleavage that was leaning over him, barely inches from his face. He noticed no rings on the fingers wrapped in her shawl, but aside from that, he resolutely kept his gaze above her neck. It wasn't exactly easy. "Do you follow all your customers out to their cars?"

Aware of the dismissive glance the man gave her chest, Sarah-Jane jerked the shawl more closely around her shoulders, clutching it together tightly with her fist. "I only follow the ones who've been drinking and want to drive." She managed to keep her voice cool, which was a feat since she'd never done such a thing in her entire life. But she certainly wasn't going to let down Maria and Jose Mendoza.

The handsome man frowning up at her had held court at the bar with his companions for hours. She didn't even want to contemplate the restaurant's liability if he drove while intoxicated.

Although, she had to admit, even in the dim light, he didn't exactly look intoxicated.

And then, he planted his foot on the ground and slid out from behind the steering wheel to stand in front of her.

She swallowed hastily, taking a step back, only to feel her ankle wobble in the high heel.

His hand shot out and he steadied her. Even adding the toe-pinching stilts to her five-foot-seven height, he was still a few inches taller than she was. And his shoulders were so wide, they actually made her feel like hers weren't.

"I think you might be the one who needs a cab."

He was laughing at her. She jerked her elbow away and took another careful, nonwobbling, step back. "The pavement's uneven," she defended, then wished she'd kept her mouth shut.

"Then you'd better be careful," he warned lightly. He looked down at her feet. "It'd be a crying shame if something happened to one of those beautiful ankles of yours."

Definitely laughing at her. "It'd be a crying shame if something happened to that beautiful car you shouldn't be driving," she returned.

He looked up at the pitch black sky for a moment. When he looked back down at her, his smile was right out there in the open. But before her defenses turned her completely into a block of stone, he stuck out his hand. "Wyatt Fortune. And aside from one shot and a bit of champagne, I was drinking soda all night. But I can walk a straight line if you want me to."

Sarah-Jane stared at the hand extended toward her. Okay, so she'd spent half the night inside the restaurant trying not to be caught watching him. And it really had been concern for everyone's safety that had prompted her to approach him when she'd seen the way he'd just been sitting alone so oddly in his car. He hadn't even closed his car door.

But now, the tall gift-from-the-gods-handsome man wanted to shake *her* hand? In the moment that it took to realize it, her palm managed to get sweaty. She tightened her grip around the wrap that Maria had provided in addition to the dress and shoes. If she continued just standing there like the world's biggest idiot, he'd end up thinking she was rude. Which was an impression she definitely didn't want to leave.

For Maria's sake, of course.

She swallowed and placed her hand in his. His fingers slowly curled around hers and heat zipped up her arm, past her elbow and beyond.

"That's not so bad, is it?"

It was agony. She waited a breathless moment for him to release her hand, but he didn't. Instead, he just continued looking at her, his gaze steady and seemingly sober.

"What's your name?"

Her face was flushing. She could feel the heat flooding right up through her ears. "S...Savannah." The name came out of nowhere and the heat in her face turned downright fiery.

His thumb drifted over the back of her hand. "Beautiful name. Beautiful city. Been there many times. Is that where you're from?"

Where had that name come from? "Um...no. My, um, my parents first met there." One lie. Now two. Maybe her parents had been to Savannah, Georgia, at some point in their lives, but it certainly wasn't where they'd met. That had been in good ol' Houston, where they still lived.

"So, Savannah." He drew out her name. "Why were you working on New Year's Eve and not out celebrating?"

She blamed the night air for the shiver working down her spine, rather than the way he was still moving his thumb ever so slowly against her hand. She tugged and he finally let it go. The fact that he seemed reluctant to do so *had* to be her imagination. It was all fired up because she'd spent so much of the evening daydreaming. Fantasizing that she was someone like a Savannah, and not who she really was. Plain Sarah-Jane. "My boyfriend is out of town." Another whopper. What was wrong with her?

He grimaced and shook his head. "Should have known there'd be a boyfriend. Whatever he's doing must've been mighty important."

"Why?" The question popped out despite herself.

"No man in his right mind wants to leave behind a beautiful woman like you on a night like this if he can possibly help it."

She twined her fingers tightly in the cashmere wrap. She couldn't come up with a response to save her soul.

"Are you headed home?"

She nodded.

He smiled slightly and glanced around the parking lot. Even the other two cars had now left. "Where's your car?"

"I walked."

"Ah. Can I give you a ride?"

Her mouth dried up. She shook her head even though something inside her wanted to jump up and down with glee.

"You sure?" He spread his hands. "I promise you'd be safe. Whether it looked like it or not in there, I leave most of the drinking to my brothers. I'm sober as a judge." He smiled slightly. "If we kissed, you wouldn't taste anything but me."

Her jaw loosened. *If?*

"But then your boyfriend probably wouldn't approve."

She nearly choked. Thank goodness he didn't ask for the nonexistent boyfriend's name. "No. Probably not."

"Seriously, though. You shouldn't be out walking alone at this hour."

"It's only a few minutes from here. I'll be fine."

"And getting in the car of a stranger isn't something you're anxious to do."

Her ears went hot again, because that thought hadn't even entered her mind. And it certainly should have.

"Well." He suddenly caught her hand up in his again, only to lift it and drop a kiss on the back of it. "You walk carefully, Savannah. And have yourself a good New Year." He tugged his loosened tie off completely and tossed it in the car before following it.

"You too," she finally managed faintly.

But she knew he hadn't heard.

He'd already started the engine of the expensive-looking car and was driving away.

She couldn't help feeling like she'd blown her one and only chance with the handsome man. For her *and* the nonexistent Savannah.

Chapter Two

"Why didn't you let him give you a ride home?" The next morning, Sarah-Jane's roommate, Felicity Thomas was staring at her through bleary eyes.

Sarah-Jane filled the coffee mug and nudged it toward Felicity. She'd asked herself that a dozen times already. "Wyatt Fortune is a stranger," she said with hard-won calmness. "I don't take rides from strangers."

Felicity rolled her eyes, then moaned a little, clapping a hand to her forehead. She reached blindly for the coffee mug. "He's a Fortune," she mumbled, as if that excused anything and everything. "Of course he's trustworthy."

Several hours' worth of fitful sleep might not have particularly refreshed Sarah-Jane after the unexpected encounter, but at least by the time she rolled out of bed and pulled on her running clothes, she'd regained her usual common sense. "That's what they always say after a serial killer is caught. *He seemed so trustworthy.*" Not that she really thought for a second that Wyatt Fortune wasn't perfectly trustworthy.

She nudged the coffee mug an inch to the left until Felicity's hand found it. Her roommate quickly buried her nose in the mug for a long moment, then leaned her head back against the kitchen chair where she sat. "Bliss," she sighed. "Remind me again why I thought it was a good idea to go to that 'I hate New Year's Eve' party?"

Sarah-Jane knew that Felicity had been just as desperate as she'd been for something to do the night before. In her friend's case, however, it was because her latest romance had come to a screeching halt a few weeks earlier. "None of the guys there were interesting?"

"Nobody offered me a ride home, that's for sure." Felicity sat forward again and propped her chin on her fist. A petite, blue-eyed blonde, Felicity was as different from Sarah-Jane as a person could be. She was three years younger than Sarah-Jane's twenty-seven, and she was her dearest friend. "It was depressing, frankly. I thought it would be a good way to ring in the New Year. Something different, you know?" She made a face and lifted her narrow shoulder. "Instead, it turned out to be just one big pity party. Then I ate too much. And drank too much. Like I said, depressing." She drew out the word, emphatically.

"At least you didn't go around making up names for yourself." The two roommates had no secrets from each other. Sarah-Jane had already given Felicity the embarrassing details.

"Savannah," Felicity mused, propping her chin on her hand again. "I should come up with a new truffle called Savannah. It'd be completely innocent-looking from the outside, but the second you bit into it…sly and sexy as all get out."

Sarah-Jane couldn't help but laugh. Felicity was a confectioner. It never took her long to get around to comparing the candy she made to the living things around her. "I certainly didn't feel sly and sexy last night." She topped off her coffee and for a moment thought longingly of the cream and sugar that she used to add to it. But she'd given up both months ago. Along with a lot of other things she'd dearly loved. In their place, she'd taken up steamed vegetables, lean meats and running. The result was a twenty-five-pounds-slimmer Sarah-Jane, but that didn't mean she still didn't miss that cream and sugar every single day. "I felt like an idiot. First off, wearing that dress that Maria gave me to wear—" She shook her head again.

"You looked fabulous."

"I looked like a pig stuffed in a blanket."

Even with her bloodshot eyes, Felicity looked suddenly stern. She pointed her finger at Sarah-Jane. "You did not. You have a figure a lot of women would kill for and that dress just happened to show it off. And get your mother out of your head right now."

Sarah-Jane grimaced. She was fairly certain nobody was ever standing around looking at *her* with envy. Weight loss or not, her breasts and her butt were still too big. But she knew that Felicity's comment about her mother had some bearing. Yvette Early was nothing if not critical about herself, as well as the farm-girl-size daughter she'd been despairing over for as long as Sarah-Jane could remember. "I sounded like her, huh?"

"Exactly like her."

Sarah-Jane shook her head, staring out the kitchen window of their cozy two-story apartment. Outside, the sky looked exquisitely blue.

Wyatt Fortune's eyes were that sort of blue.

"I can't believe I lied to him like that."

"Why did you?"

Sarah-Jane chewed the inside of her lip, then shrugged. "I don't know. I guess I just didn't want to be plain Sarah-Jane."

"You're not plain!"

"You grow up with a nickname, sometimes it fits."

"Not anymore, it doesn't," Felicity said loyally. "But, hey, everyone wants to be someone else now and then. Me, I'd like to be a five-ten Brazilian model." She narrowed her eyes for a moment. "Named Marguerite." Despite her pallor, her smile was quick and infectious.

"Marguerite and Savannah," Sarah-Jane returned. "Women of mystery and intrigue."

"Exactly." Then Felicity dropped her hand to the table, following it with her head, which she just laid right down next to her coffee mug. "But good ol' Felicity Thomas is never going to drink a margarita again."

"I doubt that," Sarah-Jane said dryly. But she felt some sympathy for her friend's misery and went to the upstairs bathroom they shared to retrieve the aspirin. Back downstairs in the kitchen that owed its cheerfulness more to decorative creativity than expense, she poured out a few tablets and set them next to Felicity's coffee. "Maybe you'd feel better if you had something to eat."

"I'd feel better if somebody just shot me in the head."

"What about a chocolate croissant?" Sarah-Jane suggested. Felicity could eat them until the cows came home and still be the size of a pixie.

"Oh, rats." Felicity suddenly lifted her head again. "What time is it?" She reached over and turned Sarah-Jane's wrist so she could see the face of the plain black and silver Timex. "I've got a delivery to make over at La Casa Paloma in an hour."

"Even on New Year's Day?"

"Even on." Felicity made a concerted effort to look more alert. She scrubbed her hands down her cheeks. Blinked her eyes several times. The end result was a pink-cheeked Felicity who still had bloodshot eyes and pale skin. "When Wendy Fortune Mendoza calls you up to request personalized chocolates for a New Year's Day-slash-post-wedding brunch, you don't say no." She dropped her head to her arms on the table, once more. "Holidays and hangovers or not," she finished on a groan.

"Is everything ready for the delivery?"

Felicity's answer was a flop of her hand. Sarah-Jane realized that her friend was giving a thumbs-up—just a sideways one, flat against the tabletop.

"Want me to drive you?"

Felicity lifted her head. Squinted at her. "You are the best friend. You know that?"

Sarah-Jane grinned wryly. "Works both ways. Go drag yourself into the shower. If the chocolates have to be there in an hour, we've only got a few minutes to spare. The order's at the shop, right?" Felicity's shop, True Confections, shared space with a coffee shop. It wasn't far, but it would still take up time getting there.

"Right." Felicity bonelessly slid out of her chair and headed out of the kitchen, correcting course when she bumped her shoulder against the doorjamb along her way.

Sarah-Jane quickly turned off the coffeemaker and went to her own room to exchange the robe she'd thrown on after her shower for a pair of clean jeans and the royal blue pullover sweater that Felicity had given her for Christmas. She'd wear it at least once so as not to hurt Felicity's feelings, even though Sarah-Jane considered the cashmere knit too revealing with its surplice neckline. She heard the shower go on and quickly wove her hair into a braid and went back downstairs.

Considering everything, Felicity made good time and before long, they'd made it to the shop where Sarah-Jane loaded up the backseat of her small hybrid with the lovely aqua-colored boxes containing Felicity's confections. Red Rock was never particularly troubled with hordes of traffic—except a few times a year, like during the Spring Fling that drew people from far and wide—but there were even fewer cars on the road thanks to the holiday, so it wasn't long before Sarah-Jane pulled up outside the exclusive hotel. Unfortunately, despite their rush and the brevity of the trip, Sarah-Jane's roommate had sunk ever more deeply down in her seat. It was as if she'd expended all the energy she had unlocking the shop. Now, she looked even greener than she had at home.

"Maybe I should take in the boxes," Sarah-Jane suggested.

Felicity started to shake her head, only to close her eyes and groan. "Never. *Never* drinking again."

Sarah-Jane unclipped her seat belt. "Sit tight. Where do the boxes need to go?"

"The banquet kitchen."

"Can I go through the lobby?"

"Technically, we should go around to the service entrance, but this way is three times as fast, and I'd rather have the chocolates there on time." She eyed Sarah-Jane through one slitted eye. "And you don't look like a delivery person anyway."

Sarah-Jane figured she didn't look like the kind of person who would be a likely guest at the hotel, either, but there wasn't any time to worry about it. They had only minutes to spare if Felicity's chocolates were going to make it to the dessert table on time.

After Felicity gave her the directions to the banquet kitchen, she stacked the boxes carefully in her arms and carried them into the hotel, peering over the top of them. The interior of the lobby was decorated head-to-toe in holiday sparkle and she circled around the staggeringly tall fir tree with golden glass icicles dripping from every branch that held court in the center of the space. Felicity had told her to take the hallway off the left of the elevators and she had just spotted those, when the doors slid open.

And Wyatt Fortune stepped out.

Sarah-Jane's breath stuck in her throat and her grip on her precious cargo started to slip.

It didn't seem possible, but he was even more handsome than she'd realized. Maybe it was the weathered blue sweater that stretched across shoulders that looked even wider than they had in the dark suit he'd worn the night before. Or maybe it was the glint of sunlight on his downturned head that shot sparks of gold into his dark blond hair, rivaling the tree's icicles.

He was…beautiful. And just that one sight of him made everything inside her squeeze.

He had a cell phone in his hand that he was studying and before he could see her, she whirled on the heels of her white tennis shoes and clutched the boxes tighter to her chest. The reception desk was to her right and she made a beeline for the pretty, young clerk standing at the far end.

"Excuse me," Sarah-Jane greeted her breathlessly. "Is it possible for someone from the banquet kitchen to come out and get these?" She lifted the boxes a few inches, even though there was no need. Even with the high reception desk between them, the girl could clearly see Sarah-Jane's load, but she frowned with doubt and started to shake her head. "These are special chocolates for the Fortune brunch," Sarah-Jane added quickly.

Magical words. The girl's expression cleared and she reached out her hands for the boxes. "I'll take them back myself."

Sarah-Jane gratefully passed over her load. "Thank you so much."

"Not a problem," the girl assured. She rounded the end of the desk and Sarah-Jane pretended she had tunnel vision, heading straight for the hotel entrance.

Do not look around that enormous Christmas tree, do not peek out Wyatt Fortune, do not pass go.

Her tennis shoes squeaked a little as she quickly crossed the tile floor.

"Savannah!"

Was there another Savannah? A real one?

But she knew there wasn't, because it was Wyatt's voice that had called out the name. She recognized it just as surely as she knew her own face. The automatic glass doors slid open. She could see her car just across the parking lot...

"Savannah. Wait!"

Her heart was pounding inside her chest as if she'd just run her first half marathon. She slowly turned. Wyatt was striding past the Christmas tree. Past the oversize stack of shining red-and-green-wrapped boxes circling the base of it.

She swallowed hard and pressed her moist palms down the sides of her jeans.

He stopped a few feet shy of her. He had a faint smile hovering around his lips. "Looks like you must have made it safely home from Red."

Her mouth was dry. "And you didn't wrap your car around any telephone poles."

"What are you doing here?"

She decided his eyes were more brilliantly blue than the sky. And with his gaze focused like a laser on her face, she was hard-pressed not to forget everything, including the art of speech. He must not have seen her give the boxes to the reception clerk. "I was dropping something off for a friend."

"This is a New Year's sign, you know."

"What is?"

"Running into each other." He looked over her shoulder and suddenly wrapped his long fingers around her elbow.

She practically jumped right out of her skin and felt her cheeks go hot when she realized he was only directing her out of the entryway to allow some people to enter.

"I didn't realize you were staying here." She felt foolish as she said the words. Why *would* she have known?

He hadn't let go of her elbow and the warmth of his fingers blazed through her sweater. "Whole family is. My brothers and I have a couple of suites."

She'd never stayed in a hotel the likes of La Casa Paloma. Never stayed in a hotel suite, period. But the mention of his brothers had her thinking about poor Felicity, still waiting in the car. "How are they feeling this morning?"

His gaze roved over her face. "Hungover, to say the least." His fingers tightened around her elbow. "Have dinner with me tonight."

Disbelief rolled over her. "Excuse me?"

"Dinner," he repeated. His lips tilted a little more. "You've heard of it, right?"

"But...you don't even know me."

He smiled outright. Faint lines crinkled alongside his eyes. "All the more reason to have dinner with me, sweet Savannah. That's how we'll start getting to know one another."

Savannah.

For pity's sake. In the span of minutes, she'd managed to actually forget.

"At least give me a chance to compete against the boyfriend who's foolish enough to leave you on your own."

She wanted the floor to open up and swallow her whole. "He's...out of the picture," she managed.

"Good for you. A guy like that deserves to be dumped."

"How do you know *he* didn't dump me?" She felt a bubble of hysteria catch in her chest. It was crazy. She was talking about a boyfriend that didn't even exist. And even with a nonexistent boyfriend, she'd more likely be the dumpee than the dumper. Or at the very least, the butt end of a joke.

"If he did then he's an even bigger idiot than I thought last night." His thumb roved over the inside of her arm. Through the cashmere, the small motion was exceedingly distracting. "But if you need a shoulder to cry on, I'm game."

Every word out of his mouth was disarming. "I'm not crying," she pointed out faintly.

"Even better. So, dinner?"

Better? There was no boyfriend! There was no Savannah! "I...um, I—" *just say no* "—I'd love to."

His fingers squeezed her elbow. His eyes held a smile. "Seven?"

Say no, say no, say no! "Perfect."

She didn't know how but they were suddenly standing nearly toe-to-toe. Toe-to-boot, actually. He was wearing leather cowboy boots that looked well-worn, along with the jeans and sweater. "How about brunch now, too?"

She shook her head, still trying to make sense of things. "Sorry?"

"I'm already late for a brunch I'm supposed to be at. More wedding stuff. Pretty much everyone who was at the shindig last night is there again today. Just no bride and groom. They have enough sense to go off somewhere they can be alone." His voice dropped a notch. "Come with me. Make it bearable."

She wondered if her brain had decided to take a New Year's Day holiday. Of course, he'd be attending the Fortune brunch. And she couldn't very well show her face *there*. Maria Mendoza was likely to be there. Then there was also Wendy Fortune, and a whole bunch of other women who would recognize Sarah-Jane from The Stocking Stitch. "I really can't. My roommate is waiting for me, actually. I need to get going." In fact, the need to escape this madness was almost overwhelming. She started edging for the door again and his hand dropped away.

"All right. But give me your number first. I'll call later for directions to your place."

"I'll just meet you back here," she said quickly. "It's easier. Seven. Right?"

His expression turned curious and she froze, fresh guilt swamping her. But after a moment, all he did was nod. "See you here at seven," he said agreeably.

Afraid of what other trouble her tongue would get her into, she practically ran out of the hotel. She didn't look back until she reached the car. And when she did, there was no sight of Wyatt through the glass doors.

She exhaled and dropped her forehead onto the edge of the car door.

"Everything go okay?" Despite the January chill in the air, Felicity had rolled the windows down in the car and tilted back the passenger seat until she was practically laying down.

"I guess you could say that."

Felicity shaded her eyes with her hand and looked out at her. "You didn't drop the boxes, did you?"

"No, the boxes were fine. Duly delivered." She pulled open the door and got behind the wheel. "I, um, I ran into Wyatt Fortune. He...he asked me out to dinner tonight."

Even though the action made her wince, Felicity adjusted the seat until she was sitting upright again. "And I suppose once again, you turned him down."

Sarah-Jane shook her head and laughed a little, still horrified that she hadn't. "I said yes. Not that it's going to do me any good. When he learns I didn't even give him my real name, he's going to think I'm a whack job!"

"You don't know that."

"Please." She started the car and pulled out of the parking spot. "Would you give a guy the time of day if he'd lied about his own name the first time you met?"

Felicity made a face.

"Exactly." Then she exhaled. "It doesn't matter, anyway. Truth or not, he's so far out of my league it's not even funny."

Sarah-Jane didn't even *have* a league. "It's not like I'll ever be hearing from him again after tonight, anyway," she added. The last time she'd gone out on a date, she'd still been in college. The time before that, high school. Neither episode had been even remotely successful.

"If you're so certain of that, then why not just enjoy the evening with him, *Savannah?*"

"How much do you think she knows?"

At Sawyer's question, Wyatt followed his brother's gaze. He had no need to ask who Sawyer meant. His brother was watching their mother, Clara, where she was seated across the room with their aunt and uncle. Her husband, James, might not get along with his brother, but Clara was too cultured to let that affect her behavior at a family event. After all, it was John and Virginia's daughter's wedding they were all celebrating.

Wyatt watched his mother. She was only fifty-six and looked as fashionable as ever without a single strand of blond hair out of place. A cloud had been hanging over Wyatt and his brothers ever since James had called them into his office just after Christmas to announce he was selling off the company. But not by word or deed did they have any clue if their mother knew a single thing about it. And if she didn't—which seemed to be the case—then *why* in hell hadn't their father told his own wife?

What was he hiding from her? From them all?

Wyatt hated wondering, but there was no way around it. That's what secrets did.

"We've got to tell her we're not going back today," Sawyer said.

At least they were in agreement about that. Once his brothers had finally rolled out of their beds that morning, they'd hotly argued the matter, yet again, until finally, Shane—

hangover and all—had stormed out of the suite, effectively ending his part of the discussion. He'd eventually returned in enough time to get ready for the brunch, but Wyatt knew his eldest brother was still struggling hard with the situation.

Wyatt wanted to understand their father's actions, too. But he wasn't willing to go back and *hope* that James would be more forthcoming about his decision. Their father had said what he'd had to say and as far as Wyatt was concerned, that was that.

At least Asher was hanging tough, and in Wyatt's opinion, he had the strongest reason to want to return to Atlanta. Atlanta was the only place that his four-year-old son, Jace, knew as his home. Wyatt figured that the little boy would adjust. He had a father who doted on him, after all.

Sawyer was iffy, though, hovering somewhere between Asher's cautious agreement and Shane's outright reluctance. Even now, Shane was glaring at the plate of food in front of him as if he wanted to kill his scrambled eggs dead.

When their mother hugged Virginia before heading purposefully toward their table, Sawyer picked up his coffee mug. "Here she comes."

"Staying in Red Rock was your idea, Wyatt," Asher reminded, more than a little dryly. "I say you can break the news."

Shane muttered an oath and pushed away from the table, altogether.

Wyatt watched him leave. "*What* is with him?"

"He's been crabbier than ever since he got in this morning," Sawyer dismissed. "Maybe he didn't have any luck with the brunette he was trying to hook up with when we got back to the hotel after the reception. But speaking of hooking up— what happened with that hostess from the restaurant that you couldn't stop looking at?"

Before Wyatt could tell his brother about running into

Savannah right there at their hotel, their mother arrived at their table.

"All right." She propped her hands on her slender hips. "You've all been huddling here for two hours, looking like you want to kick a dog. Now what's going on?"

Asher lifted an eyebrow, looking at Wyatt. Sawyer hid his nose again in his coffee mug. Brave brothers.

"We're not going back to Atlanta today," Wyatt said baldly.

Clara's eyebrows rose. "Then, when?" Her gaze went from Wyatt's face to Asher's. Then Sawyer's.

"We're not going back, period," Wyatt clarified.

Clara paled a little, looking pained. She closed her hands over the back of the chair that Shane had abandoned. "This has to do with your father, doesn't it." It wasn't so much a question as a statement.

"You could say that," Asher finally said.

"And Shane?"

"He's in agreement," Wyatt said with a shade more optimism than he felt.

Clara sighed and sat down in the chair. "I knew there was something going on between all of you. James—" She shook her head, her gaze turning faraway for a moment. "I know something's been bothering him, too."

"He hasn't told you what he's planning for JMF?"

"Just that he's making some changes." Her gaze focused on Wyatt's face again. "Long-overdue changes, is how he actually put it."

Even though Wyatt had strongly suspected his mother was in the dark, confirmation still felt like yet another blow and he forgot all about trying to couch the situation in gentler terms. "Selling JMF out from underneath us is a little more than a *change*."

"Selling!" Her eyes widened with shock and it took her a

moment to gather herself. "I'm sure your father has a reason for what he's doing," she finally said.

"I'm sure he does," Wyatt returned flatly. He wondered if his mother would so staunchly defend her husband if his mysterious reasoning ever did come to light. "He just hasn't bothered sharing with us—not even Shane," he added for emphasis, "what that reason is. It's cut and dried, Mom. Dad doesn't trust us to run JMF. I'm not going to hang around and watch him pull apart everything we've always worked for."

"And I suppose your stubbornness has convinced your brothers? Honest to Pete, Wyatt. You were born just as stubborn as your father."

"Wy's stubborn, all right," Sawyer agreed. "But Dad's the one who's cut us all out of the loop."

Clara clasped her hands together. "I've never gotten involved with JMF and I refuse to take sides here when I don't know the entire story."

"Good luck with that," Wyatt muttered.

"So you're just staying here in Red Rock? I'm going to lose you all, simply because of some disagreement you've had with James?" Disbelief knitted her brows together.

"Maybe it's time for us to make new starts," Asher said a little more gently. He glanced meaningfully across the room where his little boy was chasing around with the handful of other children there. Jace had spent the night with their little sister, Victoria, and her new husband out at their ranch, and looked happy as a pig in clover right now with his new posse.

Clara looked toward Jace, too. She blinked hard and Wyatt felt like a heel. But it was their father who had created the situation, not him and his brothers. After a moment, Clara cleared her throat. She sat up straight and eyed them. "If James wants to sell his company, that's his right," she said quietly. "We're still a family and I expect all of you to remember that."

He couldn't say he was surprised by her stance. And if

he weren't so furious with his father, maybe he'd even wish someday for a woman to stand as firmly by him.

But he *was* furious.

He looked at his mother. "Yeah, well. Why don't you give Dad that reminder when you get home?"

He half expected her to stand him up.

But when Wyatt stepped off the elevator that evening right on the dot of seven o'clock, he immediately spotted Savannah perched on the edge of one of the deep chairs dotting the lobby.

For the first time since the brunch, he felt his tension slide away. He forgot the ache that had held his head in a vise. He forgot the knot between his shoulders.

She was here.

Savannah wasn't facing the elevator and for a moment, he had a chance to observe her profile, unnoticed.

She looked nervous.

He'd figured out the night before that he made her nervous. Running into her in the lobby that morning hadn't changed his opinion. Seeing the way her fingers anxiously twisted the gold chain of the little brown purse on her lap was the nail in the coffin. That's why he'd warned himself not to be surprised if she'd ended up blowing him off.

But here she was.

And he didn't want her to be nervous.

He just wanted *her*.

He crossed the lobby, and at the sound of his bootsteps, she looked his way. Her dark eyes looked mysterious and she pushed out of the chair, tucking her lustrous, curling hair behind one ear. He'd known it would be long, and it was, hanging gloriously halfway down her back. His fingers actually twitched, imagining how it would feel.

"You're here," she said when he reached her.

He couldn't help smiling a little. "Did you think I wouldn't show?"

She lifted one shoulder. "The thought had occurred."

The night before, she'd worn a black dress that clung to every curve. Tonight, she was wearing a loosely fitted white blouse tucked into a dark brown skirt that swirled around the calves of her leather boots. The outfit was practically severe in comparison to the dress the night before, and visibly too large for her, but she was no less attractive. "Looking forward to this evening has been the only good part of this day."

She gave him a curious look, but didn't give voice to it. He touched the small of her back and headed toward the door. "I thought we'd drive to San Antonio," he told her when they left the bright lobby for the star-studded evening. "I got reservations at an Italian place on the River Walk that my cousin Wendy recommended."

"I haven't been to the River Walk since I was in college."

"What was that? Two years ago?"

Despite the dark sky, he could see the way her cheeks flushed. "Hardly," she scoffed. "I'm twenty-seven."

"So ancient," he teased gently. One way or another, he was going to get this woman to relax. "I've got two years on you. What did you study?"

Sarah-Jane could hardly think straight. Wyatt looked like he'd stepped out of the pages of some movie star magazine. And if his stupefying good looks weren't enough, his fingers were burning a hole right through to her spine. Every inch of her was tingling. "I got my MBA from the University of Texas at Austin."

"Impressive." His hand left her back and he gestured. "I'm parked over there."

The same car that he'd had at Red was parked next to a stuccoed planter that was overflowing with flowers. She was vaguely surprised that he didn't use the valet parking. But then again, when she thought about those well-worn boots he'd had on that morning, maybe it wasn't so surprising after all.

Wealthy and gorgeous or not, something about Wyatt struck her as decidedly down-to-earth.

Then she reminded herself that "Savannah" would at least know how to carry on a conversation with a handsome man. "What, uh, what did you study in school?"

"Besides the girls?" He grinned crookedly. "Finance at MIT."

"Impressive," she returned.

The parking lot light made his hair shine like gold and his eyes crinkled as he opened the door for her.

Sarah-Jane sank into the passenger seat. She knew it was silly, but she was stupidly charmed by the action. Nobody had ever opened her car door for her before.

Savannah, on the other hand, probably had doors opened for her all the time.

Just be Savannah for a night, she reminded herself. One night. And then the fantasy could end. *Would* end.

Her hand swept over the leather seat next to her legs. She was having a hard time keeping her gaze from creeping back to him. "Nice car."

"It'll do for a rental."

The fine leather put to shame her economical cloth seats. She wondered what sort of car he drove at home, but didn't want to ask. With her luck, he'd think she was only interested in his possessions and the truth was, she didn't give a lick what he drove.

"So tell me what an MBA is doing playing hostess at Red?"

Sarah-Jane wanted to cringe. *What a tangled web we weave...* "It's a job," she evaded and wondered if he were to know the real truth if he—like most people—would think she was wasting her degree working at The Stocking Stitch.

"I overheard you at Red, you know. About staying in Red Rock. I wasn't trying to eavesdrop."

"But you are trying to change the subject." He gave her an amused glance that she could see despite the darkness. "What'd your mama teach you about men? That they like mystery?"

Sarah-Jane didn't even want to think about her mother just then. "Do they?"

He slowed at a stoplight and looked into her eyes.

Her breath stopped in her chest all over again.

His voice seemed to drop a notch. "Let's just say I'm beginning to see the appeal."

Chapter Three

The drive to San Antonio seemed to fly by, giving Sarah-Jane's certainty that the evening would be a disaster little time to abate. By the time they were shown to their linen-covered table on a veranda overlooking the river, she was so tense that she wasn't sure she'd even be able to eat.

She should just tell him the truth and forget all this Savannah nonsense. He'd be disgusted, sooner rather than later. But she could go home and start pretending she'd never uttered that stupid lie in the first place. She'd be free to go on conjuring fantasies in her mind that would never come to life.

"Nice view," Wyatt murmured when he held out her chair for her. His voice seemed to whisper against her temple.

A shiver danced down her spine and she quickly looked out the wall of windows next to their table as she sat.

This time, she caught her breath without Wyatt's help at all. The view outside wasn't just nice.

It was spectacular.

Every tree seemed decked out in sparkling lights—every

color of the rainbow, it seemed—and the reflections exploded in the river water like dazzling fireworks. "It's magnificent." For a moment, she actually forgot herself, and imagined working that liquid brilliance into a knitting pattern. She looked up at Wyatt, only to find him looking at her, and not the view. His gaze was steady, that faint smile he seemed to often wear playing around the corners of his lips.

The table was clearly meant for two. Small and round, with a squat white candle inside a clear, heavy glass vase burning in the center of it. Beneath the pristine white linen covering the table, she was afraid her clumsy legs would bump right into Wyatt's.

Her nerves ratcheted right back up.

She twisted her fingers around the purse chain. Felicity had loaned it to her seeing how Sarah-Jane's usual oversize leather satchel was more suited to toting knitting projects back and forth to the shop than it was accompanying Wyatt Fortune out to dinner. Considering how fancy the restaurant was, she was glad she'd submitted to Felicity's advice. As it was, she still felt underdressed. Wyatt's black sweater and trousers had probably cost a fortune. She'd had her outfit for at least five years and it had been a clearance item, even then.

He looked like her every fantasy come to life, while she was just a fraud. She suddenly pushed out of the chair, clutching her purse to her middle.

His eyebrows shot up and he half pushed out of his own chair. "Are you okay?"

Her cheeks were on fire. She nodded. "I, um, I'm just going to visit the ladies' room."

His expression didn't really change, but he subsided in his chair. "How about if I order some wine?"

She nodded, her feet edging away from the table. Some portion of her mind wondered how much it would cost to take a cab from San Antonio back to Red Rock.

"You have any preference?"

Wine. He was talking about wine. "Whatever you choose," she said quickly. What she knew about wine wouldn't fill a thimble, but consuming some couldn't possibly make the evening any worse. She moistened her lips, more certain than ever that she was acting like the biggest fool on the planet. "Excuse me." She didn't wait for him to say another word before she fled.

Mercifully, the ladies' room was empty and Sarah-Jane clutched her hands around one of the hammered copper sinks, drawing in a deep breath. She stared at her reflection in the mirror. "Get a *grip*," she muttered.

Wyatt Fortune wasn't a high school boy bent on winning a bet with his friends by not only getting the most unlikely girl to the prom but bedding her after. He was a grown man and for some reason, he wanted to spend the evening with her.

One evening. Her one chance in twenty-seven years to pretend she wasn't plain Sarah-Jane.

She knew she had two choices. Either go with the flow...*be* Wyatt's Savannah for just one evening. Or tell him the truth and end this before it went a moment further.

Her conscience would be appeased if she did the latter. The rest of her would regret it for the rest of her life if she didn't do the former.

Savannah. It was just a name, she reasoned, much as Felicity had reasoned when she'd been frantically trying to prevent Sarah-Jane from calling Wyatt at his hotel to cancel.

The restroom door swung open, startling her, and two laughing women entered. "Who cares if it's just one night," the first woman was saying. Her gaze skipped over Sarah-Jane as if she were invisible. "It's a brand new year and I'm starting it off by having some fun." She pushed through one of the full-length doors to the first stall and her friend disappeared behind another.

Sarah-Jane's brown eyes stared back at her in the mirror. For her entire life, most people treated her as if she were invisible.

Wyatt didn't look at Savannah as if she were invisible.

She snapped open her purse and ran a fresh layer of pale gloss over her lips. Then she washed her hands. And pulling her shoulders back, she went back out to join Wyatt.

Sarah-Jane would never have the chance to live the fantasy.

But tonight, Savannah was going to live it for her.

Wyatt breathed a little easier when he spotted Savannah returning. He half rose until she was seated again and then lifted the wine bottle questioningly.

"Please." She nudged her empty wineglass closer to him and he poured a measure before setting the bottle aside.

"I hope you like Italian."

"I like food, period." Her lips twisted as she looked out the windows and took a sip of the wine. "Mmm." She gave him a quick look as if surprised. "It's good."

He didn't drink much, but he could still pick out and enjoy a decent wine. "Glad you like it."

She ducked her nose in the goblet, quickly looking back out the windows. He dragged his eyes away from the long line of her throat. Her blouse was so loose, it was starting to slide toward her shoulder.

"It looks like every tree has lights," she mused.

He was a lot more interested in looking at her than at the trees. "Savannah?"

Again, that enticingly quick glimpse of chocolate brown before her lashes swept down again. "Mmm?"

"Do I make you nervous?"

He saw her long fingers tighten around the stem of her wineglass. Her fingernails were short, neat and polished in the faintest of pink. He found them strangely vulnerable-looking.

And enticingly sexy. The last woman he'd briefly dated had sported talons painted deep purple. She'd been mildly entertaining, and *never* nervous. But if he had to think of her name just then, he'd have been hard-pressed to do so.

On the other hand, there was something about Savannah that was entirely unforgettable.

"Maybe a little nervous," she finally admitted when he just waited, silently. She made a face. "You must think I'm silly."

"I don't think you're silly," he assured. "I do think I'm glad you're with me instead of the other guys here who are wishing you were with them, instead."

She gave a breathy, disbelieving laugh. "Did your mother send you to charm school or something?"

He smiled. His mother had left for Atlanta that afternoon as planned; but he seriously doubted she was charmed by anything he or his brothers had said before she'd departed. "No doubt she's wanted to try, more than once." He saw the waiter approaching from the corner of his eye and gave him a quick look. The waiter immediately veered off, heading for another table.

Smart waiter. Good tip.

Wyatt topped off her wineglass before setting the bottle aside once more. He wasn't trying to get her drunk. He just wanted her to get over her nervousness. He lifted his own wineglass, watching the way the liquid clung to it when he swirled it a few times before lifting the glass to his lips.

"I thought you didn't drink."

"I don't worry about trying to keep up with my brothers," he corrected. He set the glass on the table. His fingertips were barely an inch away from hers. He saw the way her gaze flicked down to the table and wondered if she was noticing that as well. "Do you have any siblings?"

"I wish." Seeming to regret her fervent reply, she shifted in her chair. Even in the subdued lighting, he could see the flush on her cheeks. "But no. No brothers or sisters. And you have—" She lifted her eyebrows. "Four brothers, I'm guessing?"

"Three brothers. The dark-haired guy next to me last night was my cousin, Michael. I've also got a little sister. Victoria. She lives in Red Rock, too."

Savannah was nodding as if she'd just realized. "That's right. She's married to Garrett Stone."

"I keep forgetting what a small town Red Rock is. You know them?"

She quickly shook her head. "Not really. I just had a stu— A friend who had to find a home for her dog once, and I remember her saying that Garrett had taken the pet in for her."

"That sounds like Garrett all right." He wondered what she'd been about to say. Wondered why she hadn't. "Still seems strange to think of Vic as a married lady. She's the baby of us all."

"And you?" She shifted in her seat, sitting closer to the table. He liked to think, closer to *him*. "Where do you fall in the line?"

"Smack in the middle."

"What's that like?"

"Frustrating when I was a kid." He grinned wryly. "I was either old enough to know better, or too young to do it." At least that got her to smile. "Sawyer's younger than me, Asher and Shane are older," he added.

"I don't know what it's like being a middle child, but it must have been great growing up in a large family like that. You and your brothers—and your cousin—looked pretty close last night at Red."

"Close in some ways, but we don't feel like we have to live in each other's pockets, either."

"Yet it sounded like you've all made the decision to move to Red Rock?"

"For not eavesdropping, you picked up a lot."

She colored again, so prettily that he couldn't help but smile. Nor could he help sliding his fingers through hers and giving her hand a gentle squeeze. "I'm teasing."

Her eyes looked startled, but she didn't pull away. "I suppose with that many brothers plus a sister, you grew up with a lot of teasing."

His smile grew. He slowly rubbed his thumb over the base of her wrist, feeling the smooth, tender skin as well as the pulse fluttering there. "Believe me, Savannah. I'm not feeling at all brotherly to you."

Her gaze met his for an instant, danced away shyly, then danced back again. "I'm glad to hear it."

He realized he was staring at the soft curve of her lips. He seriously wanted to taste them. But they were in the middle of a busy restaurant. And he damn sure didn't want to scare her off just when she was starting to lose that tight aura of tension she wore wrapped around herself like a winter coat.

"Soooo." He reluctantly slid his hand free and picked up one of the thickly padded menus the waiter had left while Savannah had been in the restroom. "What are you hungry for?" He handed her the menu.

In the flickering candlelight, her dark eyes seemed to grow even darker. She took the menu from him, but left it unopened. "Everything looks good to me."

"You're not looking at the menu."

Her cheeks were pinker than ever. But her voice sounded throaty. "I know."

He choked back half a laugh and shifted in his chair. Damned if he wasn't more turned on by her right then than if she'd been stark naked and tucked beneath him. He grabbed the menu and flipped it open, staring blindly at the selections, very well aware that this time, she was the one silently observing him. He decided it was strangely humbling.

Fortunately, as if he could tell that Wyatt didn't want to keep him at bay any longer, the waiter returned, bearing a plate of bruschetta that he set in the middle of the table. Savannah didn't dally over ordering like so many women seemed to, choosing seared sea bass over eggplant. When the waiter turned inquiringly to Wyatt, he handed back the menu. "Pepperoni pizza."

Savannah laughed softly. "We could have had that easily in Red Rock. I think I've over-ordered."

Because he couldn't resist, he took her hand again, sliding his fingers through hers. "What can I say? I like the simple pleasures in life. And, besides, Wendy recommended the pizza. Says it's the best pie this side of Chicago." He leaned toward her. "Don't worry," he murmured. "I'll share."

A bubble of laughter escaped her lips and she clapped her free hand over her mouth.

He smiled. "Don't do that. I like hearing you laugh."

She lowered her hand but only to reach for the wine bottle, which she tipped over her emptied glass. "My mother would sorely disagree," she told him lightly. "She says I laugh like a horse."

What kind of mother told her daughter that?

His thoughts went black.

Maybe the same kind of father who raised his sons to be part of something lasting, only to snatch it away with no warning. "Better a hearty laugh than a miserly one," he told her.

Savannah peered at him through narrowed eyes, but she was still smiling. "Now that sounds like charm school again to me."

"Nothing charming about the truth." Until recently, Wyatt would have said he'd learned everything there was about *truth* from his father.

"Definitely nothing charming about the truth," Savannah agreed, "when the truth isn't pleasant."

He shook his head, drawn back out of the darkness by the wry curve of her supple lips. "That's not what I meant at all." He dropped a kiss on her knuckles and felt her go still. But after a half a moment, she relaxed again and reached for her wine.

By the time the waiter returned with their meals, Savannah was laughing unselfconsciously enough not to try to hold it back or cover it up with her hand. And even though Wyatt tried to offer her a piece of the pizza—which was just as good as Wendy had promised—she waved it off. "I'll stick with the fish," she said firmly. "If I start eating that stuff again, I'll never want to stop."

"I see the way you're eyeing it." He waggled a piece above the flickering candle. "I recognize hunger when I see it."

She just gave him a look from beneath her lashes. "Who says I'm looking at the pizza?"

He gave an abrupt laugh and dropped the pizza back on his plate. "You're dangerous with a little wine in you."

She smiled slightly, looking like the cat who'd gotten the cream. He had a strong hunch that it was not a feeling she'd had very often and he couldn't help wondering about her even more. And thinking that he wouldn't mind being the reason she had that expression on her face more often.

When they'd finished their wine and their food, Wyatt asked if she wanted to hurry back to Red Rock or explore the River Walk. She didn't hesitate. "Explore."

So he took her warm hand in his and they set out on foot. They stopped and listened to a jazz band playing in a crowded little club; they walked over an arched bridge where Savannah stopped to hang her arms over the stone side and stare down at the lights reflected in the water; and when she grew chilled in the steady breeze, he pulled her into a boutique that was open for business despite the holiday, and bought her an ivory-colored wrap.

"Like this," the shopkeeper instructed in her slightly accented English, and dropped the wrap over Savannah's auburn hair, tossing the long ends around her shoulders with casual elegance.

For a second, Wyatt imagined Savannah in ivory with a different sort of veil drifting from her lustrous hair.

He yanked out his wallet and paid for the thing, banishing the absurd thought from his head.

Blissfully, Sarah-Jane wandered around the shop for a few more minutes before Wyatt took her hand again, and they set off once more. After the shop, they followed the pathways, still with no clear destination in mind. He talked her into sharing chocolate-covered strawberries at an open-air café, only because she couldn't seem to resist anything he suggested. They wandered into and out of clubs, listened to comedians and even wove their way onto crowded dance floors though she knew she couldn't dance a lick.

Every time she started to feel her insecurities come to the fore, she simply asked herself what *Savannah* would do.

It was clearly Savannah whom Wyatt was interested in, and Sarah-Jane felt herself more and more slipping into the part. She didn't jump out of her skin when he slid his arm around her shoulder and held her close as they crossed over bridges, from one side to the other. And she flirted.

Oh, how she flirted.

And as she drank Irish coffee in a pub, cheering him on in an impromptu game of darts, then another glass of wine in a dark little shop where a man in one corner was rolling cigars, it just got easier and easier.

And when they crossed another bridge, and he tugged her into his arms when they were on the top of it, swirling her around in a slow dance, she tossed her head back and stared up at the sky, not entirely certain where the lights from the trees ended and the stars began.

"This is the mos' perfect night I've ever had," she told him, vaguely aware of the way her words slurred…just a little… and not caring one whit. "Cinderella's got nothin' on this."

He just smiled indulgently and tucked his arm around her, holding her close against his side. His breath was warm against her ear. "Fortunately, your carriage didn't turn into a pumpkin at midnight, either."

She shivered and knew it was owed strictly to him. "An even more perfect fantasy," she sighed happily. She looked up at him, blinking a little until her vision seemed less wobbly. "Thank you for not standin' me up."

He laughed softly. "Honey, no man in his right mind would stand you up. And I've been accused of a lot of things, but never for not being right-minded."

"Everything about you is right." She dropped her head on his shoulder and heard him laugh all over again.

"Think you can make it back to the carriage, Cindy?"

"Mmm-hmm. 'S long 's you keep your arm around me." She turned her head a little, nuzzling into the space between his shoulder and his neck that seemed to have been made just for her. "You smell so good," she murmured. Like coffee, she thought hazily. Coffee and chocolate strawberries and wishful dreams.

"And you'd tempt a saint," he returned under his breath. "You ready to head back?"

She nodded and he shifted directions yet again. Her head was swimming, but it never once occurred to her to worry about him finding their way back to his car. And almost before she knew it, he was leaning over her as she sank down in the luxurious leather seat once more, clipping the safety belt across her before closing the passenger door and going around to the driver's side. The next thing she knew, they were flying along the highway, nothing but his headlights cutting through the dark night. San Antonio was long behind them. Red Rock yet to be reached.

She eyed him in the dim light cast by the dashboard. "This is the best time I've ever had." She hadn't even realized the thought swirling inside her head had made it past her lips until she heard her own voice.

She felt his glance. Imagined that he smiled tenderly. "Me too."

She sighed sleepily. "You're a nice man, Wyatt Fortune, but you don't have to say that."

"I'm not always a nice man," he countered. "But I am one who doesn't say things he doesn't mean." He found her hand and lifted it, kissing her knuckles.

"What have you ever done that wasn't nice?"

He chuckled softly. "Besides picking on my kid brother and sister because I usually couldn't get away with it with my older brothers?"

"Just when you were children, I'll bet. Your family probably all think you're perfect."

He released her hand and shifted his hold on the steering wheel. "Not exactly."

She was sorry that he'd let go of her hand. She tucked it inside the sinfully soft wrap he'd purchased for her. She knew her yarns, and the fiber was exceptional.

She was also glad she hadn't seen the price tag on it. She could guess its value, and she would have had to refuse such an extravagance. She should have refused it.

She couldn't help but glide her fingertips back and forth against the soft ivory. Yawning, she snuggled her chin deeper into the luxurious weave. The gift had probably not meant a thing to him, but she'd treasure it. "Always," she murmured.

Wyatt heard Savannah's murmur, though he couldn't make out what she'd said. But one glance told him that she'd fallen asleep, her hands clutching the wrap like a child's favorite blanket. He smiled and slipped a lock of hair away from her cheek.

Her hair felt like cool silk; her skin like warm satin. It was hard not to get distracted wondering what the rest of her would feel like.

He soon reached the lights of Red Rock, and slowed as he drove through town toward his hotel. Savannah didn't stir, even when he pulled into the parking lot and turned off the engine. "Savannah, honey. We're here." He brushed his thumb along her cheek.

Her eyes flickered open just enough for him to see a glimmer of liquid chocolate. "Hmm?"

"Time to wake up," he murmured softly. "Give me your address so I can drive you home." The disadvantage of plying her with wine so she'd relax was that he wouldn't take advantage of the situation, no matter how appealing she was. He had some standards, and that was an unbreakable one.

"You don't have to drive me home," she said, her eyes closing once more. "My car's here."

He stroked her cheek again. "And you're in no shape to drive." Unlike the night before when she'd suspected he shouldn't drive, he knew for a fact that she *couldn't.* Nor was he about to let her try. "You live near Red, right? Savannah? Or would you rather stay here with me?"

Her eyes opened wide. She sat bolt upright, scrubbing her hands down her cheeks. She stared around, taking in the fact that they were parked outside the hotel. "Stay?"

There was no missing the shock on her face. You'd have thought she'd never spent the night with a man before. "I'll even take the couch," he offered. He knew it was the only way he'd be able to keep from touching her, no matter what his personal code demanded. But come later, all bets were off. "I'd carry you inside, but I don't want the night staff in the lobby to get the wrong idea."

Pulling her thoughts together was almost more than Sarah-Jane could manage. Wyatt had asked her to stay.

No.

He'd asked *Savannah* to stay. Savannah, who'd flirted and danced and drank wine and fancy cocktails. Savannah, who probably did not live in an economical two-bedroom apartment furnished creatively in early attic.

There was a cab parked outside the lobby. She could see the driver sitting inside. She knew she couldn't drive her own car; she could hardly focus on Wyatt's crooked smile without seeing double. It was either tell him where she lived, or take the cab.

Or go up to his room with him.

Was there really any question at all?

"You don't have to carry me," she said instead.

His smile widened slowly and heat filled her.

Walking, however, turned out to be easier said than done. She no more climbed out of the car and inhaled a deep breath of cold air, than her head swam woozily and she started to pitch sideways.

Wyatt caught her, sweeping her close.

Sarah-Jane's hands and purse was caught between them, but her heart raced anyway. Whatever fantasy she had about feeling his mouth on hers disappeared beneath the ominous lurching of her stomach. "Maybe I should just go home." The last thing she wanted was for Wyatt to witness her getting sick. Not fantasy material at all.

Savannah would hold her alcohol better.

"Okay." He reached around her for the car door once more, but she shook her head. "Savannah, you're *not* going to drive."

"I know." She swallowed hard and gingerly turned her

head, looking toward the cab. It was still sitting there. "I'll take the cab, there."

"Still being a woman of mystery, eh?" He snugged the wrap closer beneath her chin, nudging it up so he could look in her face. "Something you don't want me to see at your place? A boyfriend who's still around, after all?"

"What? No. No, No!" She shook her head automatically, only to groan when the world swam around her. Felicity had been right. No alcohol. Never, ever again. "There's no boyfriend. I promise you." At least that was the honest truth.

"Okay." He pressed a quick kiss to her forehead, letting the matter drop. "Cab it is."

She wasn't sure if he believed her or not. But she did know that it shouldn't matter, either way. She'd allowed Savannah one night. And that night was at an end. Particularly since Sarah-Jane was in danger of upchucking all over her alternate persona.

"Just wait here." He steadied her against the side of the car before crossing the parking lot in long strides to get the cabbie's attention. Quickly, Wyatt had returned and the cab was pulling up next to her. He opened the rear door and held her arm while she tried not to make a bigger fool of herself by collapsing onto the seat. Then he crouched down beside her, tucking the wrap around her as if she were no more than a child.

"I'm sorry I ruined the evening," she said miserably.

He smiled gently and tucked a lock of hair behind her ear. His thumb brushed over her cheek and for a moment, she forgot the dangerous churning in her stomach.

"Honey, you haven't ruined a single thing." He leaned closer and she held her breath, certain that he was going to kiss her. But all he did was press his lips again to her forehead. Then he backed away. "I'll call you," he promised before he closed the door between them. He raised his hand, then turned toward the hotel.

Sarah-Jane let out a sigh, watching him go.

"Where to, miss?" The cab driver was looking at her in his rearview mirror.

She closed her eyes and gave him her address.

In seconds, they were driving away from the hotel. Away from Wyatt. Away from Savannah.

Just like Cinderella, her night of fantasy had come to an end.

Chapter Four

"No, Mother, I haven't forgotten about Dad's birthday party next week." Sarah-Jane sat at the kitchen table in her apartment, holding her cell phone gingerly to her ear. The light coming in from the window was bright and she had her head propped on her hand, her fingers shading her eyes.

"Everybody who's anybody is going to be here," Yvette said, for about the tenth time. "So at least *try* to wear something suitable."

Sarah-Jane's head pounded even harder.

The cab ride home had been mercifully brief and when the driver had stopped outside her apartment and she'd fumbled in her borrowed purse for her wallet, he'd told her that the gentleman had already covered the fare.

Gentleman. The word definitely described Wyatt. He'd been a gentleman from start to finish, right down to his promise to "call her."

"It's an outdoor barbecue, isn't it?" she asked her mother, now. "Unless you've changed your mind?"

"Why would I change my mind?" her mother asked sharply. "I've been planning this for the past six months! Honestly, Sarah-Jane. You always come up with the silliest notions. Yes, it's outdoors. But it's still going to be *tasteful*. I don't want you showing up in some dreadful old jeans and baggy T-shirt."

Everything important to her mother had to be *tasteful*. "I'll wear a dress," she promised.

She could practically hear her mother sniff. "Well, I'll have something here for you just in case."

Sarah-Jane made a face. There was a reason why she was happy to have several hours' distance between herself and her parents who still lived in the same Houston house where Sarah-Jane had grown up. "You don't have to do that, Mom. I have a perfectly good dress." She'd have to purchase it, yet, but Felicity would help. And her mother hadn't seen her in months. She had no idea that Sarah-Jane had lost a few pounds. Not that it would matter. Since she'd been twelve years old and developed breasts, her mother had been trying to fit her into clothing at least three sizes too small. As if by doing so, she could pretend that Sarah-Jane was the perfectly petite person she, herself, had always wanted to be.

"Barbara Curtis is coming. So are Tiffany and Adrianna."

"That's nice." Barbara Curtis had lived down the street from the Earlys since Sarah-Jane had been in high school. As far as Yvette was concerned, the woman—and her twin daughters, Tiffany and Adrianna—were the epitome of perfection. Sarah-Jane had no particular problem with any of them. Tiffany and Adrianna had been two years behind her in school. They'd never been unkind to Sarah-Jane back then, but they'd never run in the same circles, either. Tiffany and Adrianna had been wildly popular, for one thing. Outgoing. Beautiful.

Sarah-Jane had been everything but.

"They're bringing dates," Yvette added.

Sarah-Jane pinched the bridge of her nose. Ah. Besides the dressing tastefully, the *real* crux of the matter. "That's nice."

"Your father can set you up again with young Martin from the bank," Yvette said.

Young Martin was ten years older than Sarah-Jane and still lived with his mother. She'd gone out on one date with him. The last date she'd been on, in fact. That was three years earlier, to satisfy her parents while she'd been visiting them.

He'd talked all night about himself and had kindly offered to help Sarah-Jane choose a "real" job that didn't entail working in a knitting shop. When he'd tried to kiss her good-night, she'd turned her head and the sloppy kiss had hit her cheek instead. She'd felt like she'd been licked by a slobbering dog.

She certainly hadn't wished for a kiss from him the way she had wished for Wyatt's.

"I don't need you to set me up," she told her mother.

"Lord knows you won't come up with a date of your own. When's the last time a man asked you out?"

"Last night, as a matter of fact." As soon as she admitted it, she wished she hadn't. She didn't want to endure a grilling about it from her mother. "Are you sure you don't want me to come early and help you get ready for the party?"

"The last thing I'll need is more people under foot," Yvette dismissed, the same way she had every other time Sarah-Jane had suggested that she might need help. At last count, her mother had invited fifty people to the birthday celebration. "Where'd you go? How'd you meet? What does he do?"

"It doesn't matter, Mom. I won't be seeing him again."

"Oh, Sarah-Jane. If you'd just make an *effort*—"

"Mom, sorry to cut you off." She wasn't. Not in the least. "But Felicity's just coming in the door and her arms are full. I've gotta help." That, at least was true.

Felicity was shouldering her way through the kitchen door,

a stack of flattened True Confections boxes in hand. "Your mom?" she mouthed.

Sarah-Jane nodded.

"Hey there, Mrs. E," Felicity called out.

"Tell your friend hello," Yvette muttered. "Next week now. About one. And remember. Something—"

"—tasteful," Sarah-Jane finished. "I'll remember. Bye, Mom. Love you."

The only answer she received was the dial tone.

She hit the end button on her phone and set it down on the table, reaching over to take the top several boxes off of Felicity's wavering tower. "Thought you were going to be at the shop all day."

Felicity tumbled the rest of the boxes onto the table and huffed a lock of blond hair out of her eyes. "I've done as much as I can there. Figured I'd put these boxes together at home." Now that New Year's Eve had passed, Felicity was working up to the frenzy of Valentine's Day. "What wonderfully supportive, motherly things did Yvette have to say during this week's Sunday call?"

Sarah-Jane shrugged. "Same old, same old. I've got to buy a dress for my father's party."

"Wear the dress Maria gave you for New Year's Eve."

Thinking about New Year's Eve only made Sarah-Jane think about Wyatt. "It's an outdoor barbecue," she reminded, determined not to dwell on it. She might as well have wished to jump over the moon. "Hardly the place for a little black dress."

Grinning, Felicity plopped down on the chair opposite Sarah-Jane and cleared an area on the Formica table to begin folding one of her pretty boxes together. "Your mom's gonna die when she sees how much weight you've lost."

Sarah-Jane didn't particularly want to think about that, either. No matter what she looked like, her mother wasn't going to see her any differently than she ever had. Why *would* she? Sarah-Jane couldn't see herself any differently, either.

She reached for a box and started folding, too.

"So," Felicity said after they had each finished two boxes each. "Any call from Wyatt?"

Sarah-Jane shook her head. "I told you I didn't expect to hear from him."

"He said he'd call."

"Don't they all say that?" Admittedly, she only had a few dates squeezed under her belt, but still. Plus there was the not insignificant detail that he hadn't asked for her phone number again since that one time in the hotel lobby.

Felicity grimaced, but didn't disagree. "You could call *him*. Don't you want to see him again?"

Sarah-Jane's hands paused. "Of course I do." She looked at her friend. "*Sarah-Jane* wants to see him. The only person he knows is Savannah." She shook her head. "I should never have lied. Never gone out with him. It was all wrong."

"Did it feel wrong when he was dancing with you on top of that bridge?" Felicity reached behind her and flicked the beautiful ivory wrap that was draped over the chair behind Sarah-Jane. "Or when he gave you that?"

"It was a fantasy," Sarah-Jane said. "A perfectly wonderful fantasy. But no matter what I wish, fantasies aren't any more real than Savannah. He won't call. He doesn't know where I live. If he looks—which he won't—" she added flatly when Felicity gave her a hopeful look "—he wouldn't even be looking for me."

"I bet he will," Felicity said with a certainty that made Sarah-Jane love her, even if she didn't believe her. "You wait and see. Red Rock just isn't that big and one day, Wyatt Fortune's going to come a'calling one way or another."

A shiver skipped around inside Sarah-Jane's tummy. She appreciated the cheerleading. She really did. But no matter what Felicity predicted, Sarah-Jane just couldn't see it happening.

She'd her fantasy date with Wyatt, but now she had her feet back where they belonged.

Firmly planted in reality.

"Hi." Wyatt stopped in front of the young blonde who was manning the hostess station at Red. It was the middle of the afternoon. After the lunch rush and before the dinner rush and the girl who looked no more than eighteen was standing at her post folding dinner napkins. "I'm looking for Savannah. Do you know when she'll be on duty next?"

"Savannah?" The hostess frowned. "I'm sorry. I don't know anyone by that name."

"She was working here a few nights ago. New Year's Eve."

"Oh." The girl's expression cleared and the knot inside Wyatt's stomach eased. "She must have been one of the temps that Mrs. Mendoza hired on for that night. The restaurant was closed, you see, except for a private party."

"Right. I was here."

She dimpled. "I can ask around if you want to wait. See if anyone knows how to reach her."

"I'd appreciate it."

"Sure." She left the hostess station and disappeared into the dining area.

Wyatt exhaled and squelched the desire to pace as he waited.

He could kick himself for not getting Savannah's number. Still couldn't believe that he'd managed to let her slip out of his fingers so easily. He supposed he could understand her not wanting to give him her address. Although, considering she'd been set to come up to his hotel room, it seemed extraordinarily cautious. No matter how perfect they'd seemed to be together in San Antonio, he couldn't forget that aura of inexperience that she'd never really let go of, despite the wine and cocktails.

If he'd been thinking straight, he'd have gotten her phone number at least. Only every time he'd looked into her eyes, it was all he could do not to forget his own name.

He exhaled again, and shoved his hands in the pockets of his worn, leather jacket.

He hoped she hadn't suffered too badly with a hangover. Hoped she didn't regret going out with him at all, considering how the night had ended. He wanted to finish what they'd started.

The hostess returned. She was shaking her head even before she stopped at her station. "I'm sorry, sir. I couldn't find anyone who knows Savannah. Are you sure you've got the name right?"

He grimaced. "I'm sure." He started to turn away. "Thanks for trying."

"I could check with my manager, Marcos, and ask him, if you want," she offered. "He's not on the schedule until tonight, but I could call him."

The teenager was thinking more clearly than he was. Of course, she meant Marcos Mendoza. And his cousin, Wendy, was married to him.

"Not necessary. I can call him myself."

She smiled, probably too young to wonder why he hadn't thought of doing so in the first place. The only explanation he could think of was that Savannah had him so bewitched, he'd lost his usual common sense.

He left the restaurant and returned to his car, thumbing through the phone numbers stored on his phone. He found Wendy and dialed. She answered quickly and in the background, he could hear a child's high-pitched giggles. She put Marcos on, but he was no more help than the girl at Red had been.

"I'm sorry, man," Marcos said, talking loudly over the giggling. "Maria made the arrangements for the extra staff we brought on. If we paid her, though, we'll have the information in the office at the restaurant. I can look into it when I get there tonight."

Meaning Wyatt's impatience would have to wait. "I'd appreciate it, Marcos."

"Sure. You say you went out with her, though? And she didn't give you her number."

"I think your wife can vouch for my character, Marcos," he said dryly. "I'm not intending to stalk Savannah. I just want to talk to her."

"All right." The giggling got even louder and Wyatt imagined Marcos was holding his little daughter, MaryAnne, as well as the phone. "I'll see what I come up with."

"Thanks." He ended the call and the interior of his car seemed abundantly silent without those pealing giggles.

He turned on the radio and drove out of the parking lot. Instead of heading back to the hotel—and his brothers, who hadn't seen any reason to let him live down the fact that he had spent hours with Savannah without coming out of it with something as simple as a phone number—he drove slowly through the neighborhoods surrounding Red.

He didn't know what he expected.

To see her walking around on the tree-lined streets? He knew she didn't have a dog to walk. She'd said she had no pets. He didn't even know what sort of car to look for, because he hadn't seen what she'd driven to the hotel when she'd met him there.

Finally, as empty-handed as he'd been since he'd tucked her inside the cab the night before, he returned to the hotel.

Like it or not, he'd just have to wait.

* * *

"Sarah-Jane, do you have a moment?"

Sarah-Jane looked across The Stocking Stitch. Her boss, Maria Mendoza, was standing in the doorway of the small office located in the rear of the store where, between the two of them, they kept track of the mountains of paperwork that went into operating the knitting shop. Maria was seventy now, but despite that, her shoulder-length black hair was only lightly streaked with gray and her curvy figure was still trim.

The customary smile on Maria's face that Sarah-Jane was used to was absent, though, and a whisper of unease crept through her. "Of course."

She nudged the knitting-pattern book she had open on top of a glass display case back toward the customer she'd been helping. "I'll be right back," she told her. The woman hadn't been in the shop before, but if she developed a liking for knitting—or gossip—Sarah-Jane figured she, too, would turn into a repeat customer.

Tugging the loose hem of her beige polo shirt around her hips, Sarah-Jane crossed the shop, veering around the trio of four-sided shelving displays containing skeins of yarn in a rainbow of colors and weights that were situated along the center of the main store. She nudged one of the comfy arm chairs scattered around a work table back into place, and then stopped when she reached Maria. "Is everything okay?" She kept her voice low.

"Sí, sí." Maria smiled quickly and patted her arm as she drew her into the small office, closing the door after them. There was one desk in the center of the room with chairs on either side and a computer on top that both sides shared. Maria didn't take her usual seat, however, but leaned one jean-clad hip against the corner of the desk and waved to the closest chair. She waited until Sarah-Jane had sat down before she spoke. "I had an interesting call today from Marcos."

Sarah-Jane studied the woman's dear face. "About...Red," she hazarded, wondering what would be so important that Maria would need the privacy of the office to discuss. More often than not, any business about the Mendoza family or their friends was discussed—at *length*—among the knitting-circle chairs. Sarah-Jane generally tried not to participate, but she was well aware the store was a hotbed of gossip.

"In a way." Maria folded her arms. "Tell me, darling, how well do you know Wyatt Fortune?"

Sarah-Jane felt the blood drain out of her face. "Um...not well. Why?"

Maria smiled slightly. There was no anger on her face, just a sort of gentle amusement. "But you *did* go to San Antonio with him a few nights ago?"

Sarah-Jane shifted in the chair. That draining blood had returned with a vengeance and she could feel it climbing up her throat, spreading hotly into her cheeks. "Well, yes. I...I did."

Maria spread her hands. "Ah. All is well, then." She leaned over slightly, her dark eyes suddenly dancing. "That one is very handsome, is he not? All that dark blond hair and blue eyes. Some men might look too pretty. But not Wyatt. He is—" she broke off and waggled her hands as if that would explain it. "Very masculine, yes?"

Not sure where the conversation was going, but entirely certain that she was mortified, Sarah-Jane could only nod.

"Such broad shoulders and tall. A man like that puts his arms around you and a woman feels like a woman."

Sarah-Jane squirmed in her chair. "Maria, I don't—"

"He is looking for you, niña."

For a moment, excitement blossomed inside her. But she still shook her head. "Marcos told you that?"

Maria nodded again. She sat back, crossing her arms again. She was smiling broadly. "Marcos tells me Wyatt went looking for you at the restaurant. Why do you make it so hard for him to find you? Don't you like him?"

"Of course I like him," Sarah-Jane exclaimed. "But—"

"Then why didn't you tell him your real name?"

She flushed all over again, slumping back in the chair. "I'm sorry, Maria. I never wanted to cause you or the restaurant any embarrassment."

Maria made a face. "Embarrassment? Why should I be embarrassed?" She waved her arms again as she always seemed to do. Maria rarely expressed herself without gesturing. "You think I sent you out among all those eligible men at that wedding reception because I was worried you would embarrass me?"

Sarah-Jane stared. "What do you mean, you *sent* me?" She'd long been familiar with her boss's penchant for matchmaking. But she'd never once considered that the lively woman would turn her sights in that regard on Sarah-Jane. "You didn't think to dangle me like fish bait, did you?"

"Fish bait smells," Maria dismissed. "You are a rose, and I thought it wouldn't hurt for some people to see that."

Sarah-Jane covered her face. "I wore that dress…those shoes. Oh my God, Maria! I made an absolute fool of myself."

"Bah." Maria snorted. "You need a better mirror, niña. You looked exactly the way a lovely, shapely young woman *should* look." She smiled then, abundantly pleased with herself. "And Wyatt Fortune obviously recognized that fact. But…what I don't understand is this." She leaned her head toward Sarah-Jane again. "Savannah?"

Of course Maria had to know that Wyatt wasn't looking for Sarah-Jane, but Savannah. She covered her face again, groaning. "I knew I shouldn't have gone out with him," she mumbled.

"I'm thinking you shouldn't have told him your name was Savannah," Maria said dryly. "We would have figured out more quickly who he was searching for." But then she leaned over and firmly tugged her hands away from her face. She stared into Sarah-Jane's eyes with kindness. "Why did you tell him that?"

Sarah-Jane blinked hard as mortification tried to give way to inexplicable tears. "I…just wanted to be someone he'd be interested in. Someone other than plain Sarah-Jane."

"The only one who sees you as plain is you."

Sarah-Jane could have argued that particular point, but knew there was no reason. Maria, like Felicity, was too loyal and too good of a friend to say anything unkind. "What did Marcos tell him?"

"Nothing at all." Maria crossed her arms again, but her fingers wiggled against the long sleeve of the burgundy-colored sweater that Sarah-Jane had knitted for her for Christmas. "Marcos couldn't find any record of me having temporarily hired anyone named Savannah for the reception, so he finally phoned me. I called to speak with Wyatt myself. Just this morning, in fact."

Sarah-Jane felt herself paling all over again. "And?"

"When he described the woman he was looking for—an auburn-haired beauty with liquid-brown eyes," she said deliberately, "it all suddenly made sense."

Sarah-Jane shivered. "He said that about me?" The words were practically a squeak, but she couldn't seem to help it.

Maria smiled indulgently. "He might have added voluptuous in there, too, but I don't want to embarrass you any more than necessary."

Sarah-Jane tugged at the collar of her polo shirt, trying to ignore the nervous fluttering inside her stomach. "You told him then. That my name wasn't Savannah."

Maria waved her hands. "*That,* niña, you get to do yourself. I told him I would pass on his message." She gave Sarah-Jane a decidedly stern look.

Sarah-Jane wasn't sure if she was relieved or disappointed. It would have been so easy if Maria had taken the decision out of her hands—

But no. She sat up straighter in her chair. That would have been the coward's way out. Sarah-Jane had spent most of her life hiding among the woodwork, but that didn't mean she was entirely full of cowardice.

She owed it to Maria to be truthful with the man. He *was* a Fortune, and the Mendozas and the Fortune family were thick as thieves.

"I'll call him at the hotel," she said, only to realize she didn't even know if he was still staying at La Casa Paloma. He'd been there two nights ago, but that meant nothing.

"Here." Maria pulled a folded, pink message slip from her pocket and handed it to Sarah-Jane. "He left his cell phone number."

Sarah-Jane unfolded the paper and stared at the number Maria had written.

"Now's as good a time as any," Maria said pointedly, gesturing at the phone that sat on top of the desk next to the computer monitor.

The fluttering inside her stomach dipped dangerously. "You want me to call him *now?*"

"No time like the present. There's no deceit in you, darling. But I know that somehow, you'll convince yourself that it's better for you not to call. And you'd be wrong. He wants to hear from you, Sarah-Jane."

"He wants to hear from Savannah," she returned.

Maria leaned forward again and squeezed her chin as if she were seven instead of twenty-seven. "A rose is still a rose," she said softly. "And you'll never know if you don't pick up that phone and dial."

Sarah-Jane's eyes started burning again. "You're too good to me, Maria."

The other woman smiled and patted her cheek. "It's easy to be good to someone like you, niña." Then she slid off the side of the desk and left the office, closing the door once more behind her.

Sarah-Jane stared after her for a moment. She was almost surprised that Maria hadn't stayed just to ensure that she really did call Wyatt. But then, how could Sarah-Jane not?

Maria had probably recognized that, as well.

She exhaled deeply and flattened out the message slip on the desk.

Wyatt had looked for her.

She knew once he heard the truth, he'd still walk away. But he *had* looked for her, and she held that knowledge close for a moment, letting its sweetness warm through her.

Then she slowly reached for the phone and dialed the number, pretending that her hands weren't shaking all the while.

He answered on the third ring. "Wyatt Fortune." His voice was just as deep as she remembered, though his tone was brusque.

Her stomach clutched again. She tightened her grip on the old-fashioned telephone receiver.

"Hello?"

Afraid he'd hang up before she found the courage to get out a word, she swallowed hard past the knot in her throat. "Wyatt. It's, um, it's me."

"Savannah." The brusqueness disappeared. His voice dropped a notch, turning smooth as dark molasses. "Feels like I've been trying to find you forever."

She squeezed her eyes shut. "Maria Mendoza just gave me your message."

"I'm glad. God knows she wouldn't give me *your* phone number." He sounded more wry than put out. "Can't blame her for being protective, I suppose. She obviously figured what everyone else figures. If you wanted me to be able to reach you, you'd have given me a way to do that."

She opened her eyes again, staring blindly at the colorful skeins of yarn that skipped across the computer screen. Sarah-Jane had designed the screen saver herself. The Stocking Stitch provided the download free to anyone who wanted it, as well as a few other programs she'd created. "I didn't think of it." It was almost true. "I didn't think it would matter."

Through the phone, she could hear the low murmur of voices in the background. Wyatt's voice dropped another notch. "It mattered. But I wasn't thinking about you disappearing right out of my hands, either. You've led me on quite a chase, Savannah, and I want to see you again."

Her shaking fingers twined around the coiling phone cord. She could tell him the truth over the phone, but that was almost as bad as not telling him the truth at all. "Are you still staying at the hotel?"

"Until I get some things ironed out, I'm still staying here."

She assumed he was referring to the task of moving from Atlanta to Red Rock, though he'd been no more forthcoming about those plans during the evening they'd spent together than she had been about who she really was. "It's nearly my lunch break." She usually spent it outside at a nearby park. Alone, except for the birds that always flocked nearby, hoping for a crumb or tidbit. "I could come by and see you for a few minutes."

He laughed softly. "A few minutes is better than nothing, but I was thinking more along the lines of something more... protracted." He paused for a moment, but Sarah-Jane couldn't get any response to that past the constriction in her throat. "Lunch is good, though," he said, filling the small, strained silence. "The weather's nice. Just come and find me by the pool. We'll eat out there."

Sarah-Jane was fairly certain if she tried to force food

down, it would be to a disastrous result. She let out a strangled "okay," cleared her throat and tried again, with only a
mildly improved result.

If he noticed—and how could he not?—he was too polite to say. "So, I'll expect you in what? Thirty minutes? An
hour?" He gave a laugh that didn't sound particularly amused.
"I have no idea how far you're coming from."

You could pretty much drive to anywhere from anywhere
in Red Rock in a matter of minutes. The distance between the
shop and the resort hotel was hardly any different. "Thirty
minutes," she managed. If she waited any longer than that,
she was afraid she'd chicken out.

"See you then." He didn't linger, waiting to see if she'd
respond.

Already tired of the chase, no doubt. Who could blame
him?

Certainly not Sarah-Jane.

Wyatt had never considered himself a particularly impatient man. He knew his family considered him stubborn, and
that he supposed he couldn't deny. But stubborn didn't mean
impatient.

Yet as he waited to spot Savannah passing through the only
passageway available from the lobby to the lushly landscaped
pool area where he sat at a round, stone-surfaced table shaded
by an overhead umbrella, all he could feel was impatience.

And *worry,* an annoying voice whispered inside his head.

He ignored the voice and took a gulp from one of the
iced teas he'd ordered for them both. Just because Savannah
had sounded strained when she called didn't mean there was
cause to worry.

Then why wouldn't she let you drive her home?

Again, he ignored the voice. Just because he'd been be-
sieged by suspicions nearly every waking minute since the

day his father made his stupefying announcement about selling off JMF didn't mean he needed to be suspicious about Savannah, as well.

Maybe the boyfriend is more. A live-in lover.

He yanked out his cell phone and scrolled through the call log. The number Savannah had dialed from was the third one down and identified as "StockingSti." It was better than nothing. No matter what, he now had a link back to her.

He glanced at the passageway from the lobby but there was still no sign of her.

Maybe more than a live-in lover. A husband. Just because she hadn't worn a ring didn't mean a thing.

He exhaled impatiently and looked back at his phone. In the twenty-five minutes since Savannah had called, he'd also received a call from his mother—he'd sent it straight to his voice mail and was still feeling guilty about it—and his little sister, Victoria, who'd called to arrange lunch the next day with him and his brothers.

So far, Vic hadn't shared what she thought about them staying in Red Rock, but he figured if anyone would understand, it would be her. She was the youngest of them all, but she'd had her own battles with their father over the years until ultimately, about eight months earlier, she'd decided to make her stay in Red Rock a permanent one. Of course, that permanency had had a lot to do with the rancher she'd set her heart on marrying.

"Hi."

He nearly dropped the phone right into his iced tea glass when she spoke. His gaze flew up to Savannah's face and thoughts of his sister, his brothers and his parents slid neatly out of his head.

Her hair was pulled back in a straight, smooth ponytail that exposed the long line of her throat above the collar of her tan shirt. He noted the logo stitched over her heart—*The*

Stocking Stitch—and tried not to dwell too much on the full curves valiantly filling out the baggy shirt. He shoved the phone back in the pocket of his jacket and pushed to his feet, leaning over to kiss her cheek.

Nothing more than a brush of his lips, but he was just as aware of the way she stiffened as he was aware of the soft, warm fragrance of her hair. "I'm glad you came."

Her gaze wouldn't meet his, while her fingers just nervously tugged the hem of her too-large shirt over the hips of her khaki-colored pants.

No reason to worry? Maybe the husband comes with a set of kids, too.

"Sit." His voice was a little harsher than he intended and he saw the way she flinched a little. "Please," he added more gently, and pushed out the chair next to his.

She sat and her ponytail slid over her shoulder as she leaned forward to scoot her chair in, sliding down over the curve under that logo and beyond.

He dragged his gaze up again. He'd always been a leg man. Long, lean legs usually attached to long, lean women. God knew there hadn't been a thing wrong with Savannah's beautifully curved legs in the dress she'd worn that night at the wedding reception, but he was finding the rest of the curves she possessed almost embarrassingly mesmerizing.

He was a twenty-nine-year-old-man, not a zit-faced boy who'd just discovered the wonders of women's breasts.

And dammit, she'd noticed, too. He knew it not only by the pained look in her brown eyes, but the way she hunched her shoulders forward in the loose shirt as if she could hide that God-given blessing.

He thought about apologizing, but in truth, he wasn't sorry for appreciating her beauty. And he suspected that bringing more attention to that fact would only embarrass her even more.

"So." He looked her straight in the eyes. "Let's just get it out of the way, okay? What is it that you're hiding, Savannah? A husband? Half a dozen kids? Just tell me what it is, and then we'll deal with it."

Chapter Five

Sarah-Jane's jaw went loose. "*What?* I don't have a husband!" She struggled to bring her voice down to its normal register. "I don't even have a boyfriend. I told you that already!" Today, his eyes were lighter than the sky, she thought inanely, and they were boring a hole straight through her.

She snatched up the iced tea glass that was obviously meant for her and sucked down a third of it before setting it back on the round coaster bearing a line drawing of the resort.

"Then what *are* you hiding? If you weren't interested in seeing me again, you could have just said so." His lips tilted almost charmingly, except he didn't look at all amused. "I wouldn't have liked it, but I'm a grown man. I would have accepted it and left you alone."

"I don't want you to leave me alone," she said faintly. There was nothing at all about him that didn't shout "grown man," from the strong column of his throat rising from the unbuttoned neck of his charcoal-colored shirt to the hewn angles of his jaw.

He'd exhaled as if he'd actually thought for a second she'd have felt otherwise, and covered her hand with his. "Then, tell me, Savannah. Why do I have the strong sense that you're trying to avoid me?"

The sunlight was unrelenting. She could see faint tan lines weaving out from his brilliant eyes and the distinct shadow along his jawline, as if he hadn't shaved that morning. She looked down at his hand covering hers. His fingertips were long and blunt-edged, the nails cut short. No "man"-icures for him. Just a plain-old nail clipper, she suspected. The same kind as the one she kept at home in her apartment.

Just tell him. The words seemed to scream through her head. "I've been lying to you." She pushed out the words.

His hand didn't move on hers, but she felt his stillness. "About what?"

She felt her shoulders bowing forward and made herself sit up straighter. "About everything." Her voice turned hoarse and she reached for the iced tea again.

His hand fell away from hers as she did so. He slid a pair of aviator-style sunglasses out of his jacket and pulled them on.

She felt herself quailing and took another deep drink of tea, only to cough a little as it went down the wrong way.

He didn't move. Just continued watching her, his lips unsmiling, his eyes no longer visible. His hair was brushed ruthlessly back from his face, looking more brown than blond despite the sunlight angling around the ivory market umbrella shading the table. "My name isn't really Savannah," she said huskily. "It's just Sarah-Jane."

His eyebrows tugged together, but beyond that, he made no response.

"Just plain, plain Sarah-Jane. Sarah-Jane Early." There. It was out. Soon, she'd be able to escape.

The impassive darkness of his sunglasses shifted as he tilted his head slightly. "And…?"

She lifted her shoulder and shook her head. "And…nothing. That's it. I'm Sarah-Jane and I'm Maria Mendoza's assistant manager at The Stocking Stitch." She plucked the embroidered logo on her shirt once and dropped her hand back to the table, circling the nearly empty glass. "She owns the shop and I was doing her a favor the other night at Red, filling in during the wedding reception."

He shifted in his chair and his distressed leather jacket fell open, revealing even more of the charcoal shirt stretched across his hard chest.

Maria had it right. Wyatt Fortune was *very* masculine. And very, very attractive.

She pulled her gaze away to stare into her iced tea. She lifted her leaden shoulders. "And that's it. The real me. I don't wear beautiful clothes or go to Italian restaurants or dance on walking bridges."

He cocked his head slightly and after a moment, sat forward. He nudged down his glasses and those brilliant blue eyes peered at her over the frames. "I beg to differ, Sarah-Jane. You did those things." His lips twitched. "Very well, actually."

She made herself sit very still, when all she wanted to do was squirm with discomfort. "You're just being kind."

"No," he said slowly, "I'm being honest. What I don't understand is why you felt like you had to lie about your name." He pulled off his glasses and tossed them on the table. "What's wrong with Sarah-Jane?"

He seemed genuinely confused.

She opened her mouth to answer, but nothing came. Nothing that he could possibly understand, anyway. Instead, she started to push out of the chair. "You deserved to know the truth."

"Whoa, hold on there." His hand shot out, catching her arm. "Where do you think you're running off to?"

"Back to the shop."

"You agreed to have lunch with me." He pulled gently on her arm until she subsided once more in the chair.

She eyed him. "I don't—" she broke off. Tried again. "Why would you still want to have lunch with me?"

He gave that faint smile again. "Because you have the prettiest eyes I've ever seen." Even though she'd sat back down, his hand was still wrapped around her forearm. "I really don't care what your name is, Sarah-Jane. It could be Gertrude for all I care. Savannah is a beautiful city, but I think Sarah-Jane suits you."

She grimaced. "Plain Sarah-Jane."

He squeezed her arm gently. "They used to call me Buy-it Wyatt in school."

She didn't know where the laugh came from, but it bubbled past her lips and she clapped her hand over her mouth.

"Being a Fortune isn't always easy." Something came and went in his eyes, but he still smiled. "And there's nothing plain about the Sarah-Jane I'm looking at." He finally let go of her arm and sat back in his chair. He didn't even have to lift his hand to get the attention of the waiter. The young man just seemed to materialize tableside.

"What can I get you, Mr. Fortune?"

Wyatt looked toward Sarah-Jane. She hadn't even picked up the narrow, one-page menu from where it sat in the middle of the stone table. She was looking at him, her expression baffled. Wyatt glanced at the server. "Two of the Casa salads," he ordered.

"Could you put the dressing on the side for me, please?" Sarah-Jane roused herself enough to ask.

"You bet." The boy took the menus and strode away, heading around the end of the glittering pool toward the indoor eating area.

"I have the phone number from The Stocking Stitch in

my phone now." Wyatt slid an unused white napkin toward Sarah-Jane and handed her the pen from the inside pocket of his jacket. "How about a home number? Or an address?"

She picked up the pen and, careful not to tear the casual, paper napkin, wrote out the information. "You don't have to call me or anything just to be nice," she said, nudging the items back to him.

He pocketed the pen and left the napkin next to his iced-tea glass. Once he'd seen a number, he rarely forgot it, but he liked looking at it there. Knowing that she'd offered it. It was more satisfying than having a wary kitten decide it was safe to climb in your lap. "There're plenty of folks who'd quickly tell you I'm not always nice at all."

"I doubt that."

In the bright sunshine, her eyes looked more like golden caramel than chocolate and they were almost enough to make him forget what he was saying. "Someday when you meet my brothers, you'll have proof." Much to his regret, her lashes swept down, hiding those eyes. And that wasn't going to do, at all. "What does the assistant manager of a knitting shop do, anyway?"

Almost immediately, the wary frown between her eyes seemed to ease. "Whatever Maria needs me to do," she said. "I handle inventory, maintaining it, stocking it, that sort of thing. Work with the customers, teach some classes. Maintain the website, take care of order fulfillment. Whatever comes up."

"What does Maria do?"

"Hiring and firing." She wrinkled her nose. "I've tried the firing part lately. We have a part-time girl helping out during the afternoons, but it's just not working out."

"Have you told her what the problem is?" He almost asked her what the details were since she was clearly more comfortable talking about work than herself, but figured that would be too nosy. Particularly when the person was still in their employ.

Sarah-Jane was nodding. "More than once. So far she hasn't changed her ways. Maria told me this morning that I need to let her go. I'm not looking forward to it. I know she's helping out with the bills at home. She's one of three and their mother's a single mom. Struggling." She looked troubled. "I know that's why she took—" She broke off and shook her head. "I'm sorry. I shouldn't be talking about this with you."

"You're too soft-hearted. If the girl's stealing—and yes, I know you didn't tell me that, but I'm guessing—cut her loose." Suddenly, the topic felt too close to home. His father hadn't stolen JMF from them, but he might as well have. In making his unilateral decision to sell, he'd snatched away from Wyatt and his brothers any say with the company that they'd helped run. The company they'd helped grow and become even more successful. The company they'd all believed to be their future. "Maria is right to fire her," he said, his voice flatter than he intended. "Right is right and wrong is wrong. There's no gray area in between."

"Well." Sarah-Jane looked uncomfortable. "I'd like to think that sometimes there is a reason to look for that gray."

There was no gray area where his father's actions had been concerned. Fortunately, before Wyatt could decide whether or not he wanted to debate the point with Sarah-Jane, the waiter returned and set their salads in front of them. It was a lot more pleasurable watching Sarah-Jane eat than it was thinking about his father.

He picked up his own fork and dumped half of the spicy dressing over the elaborate Tex-Mex salad. Sarah-Jane, on the other hand, used only a fraction, he noticed. "Dressing too spicy for your tastes?"

Her gaze darted almost guiltily to the silver container next to her plate. "Not at all. I'm a native Texan. I like spicy." As if to prove it, she found a piece of jalapeno pepper with her fork and popped it in her mouth. Her eyes closed, distinct pleasure suffusing her expressive features.

Heat streaked straight down his spine. He let out a breath, looking away from her face to his own salad. God help him if he ever had the opportunity to share *real* pleasure with her.

She'd eaten only about half of the salad when she started looking at her watch. "I'm going to have to get back to the shop. We have a knitting group coming in this afternoon from San Antonio." She set down her fork and dabbed the corner of her mouth with her napkin.

He gestured for the waiter. "They don't have sewing shops in San Antonio?"

"Knitting," she corrected with a smile. "And sure they do. Just none that are as fine as The Stocking Stitch. We have one group who regularly comes all the way from Dallas."

"To do what?"

She laughed softly. "Knit, of course."

"And *you* knit."

Her eyes sparkled with amusement. "Well enough to teach a few classes," she said mildly.

"I suppose your mother taught you?"

The sparkle dimmed a little. "I learned how to knit and crochet when I was away at college. The first time I picked up a pair of knitting needles I was hooked." Her smile returned. "No pun intended."

"What do you make?"

She propped her elbow on the table and rested her chin on her hand. "Why, musty ol' knit caps and scarves," she drawled dryly. "Isn't that what you think?"

He actually felt heat rise up his throat.

She chuckled. "You'd be surprised what kinds of things are hand-knitted or crocheted." She sat back when the waiter returned. Wyatt asked for the check.

"Sure thing, Mr. Fortune. Do you want me to box up the rest of your salads?"

Wyatt, who'd actually found himself wondering what surprising things there could be, started to shake his head, but Sarah-Jane was nodding. "Yes, please," she told the boy. "It's delicious, but I really have to get back to work."

"Not a problem at all." The waiter took their plates and headed toward the doors again.

"I won't have to cook anything for dinner." Sarah-Jane looked happy with that prospect.

"Save it for lunch tomorrow and I'll take you out to dinner."

Just that easily, the wary little line reappeared between her soft, brown eyebrows. "I can't. Those classes I mentioned teaching? I have one tonight. Every Tuesday and Thursday, actually."

"Tomorrow's Wednesday. What about that?"

He saw a swallow work down her throat. "I promised my roommate I'd help her at her shop tomorrow night after work."

"Another shop. Let me guess. Sewing stuff?"

The line disappeared and she smiled again. "True Confections," she said. "The most wonderful candies and chocolates you can ever imagine. I was delivering an order of them to the hotel here when you caught me New Year's morning. Your cousin, Wendy, ordered them specially for that brunch."

"Which explains why you were so anxious not to join me when I asked?"

Her gaze dropped guiltily and her nose turned pink.

"Don't ever lie," he murmured lightly, brushing his finger quickly down the fine line of her nose. "Now I know the sign that'll give you away every time."

She didn't look at him when the waiter came back bearing the take-out containers holding the rest of their meals. She thanked the boy and waited until he'd left the check portfolio next to Wyatt and departed again before her gaze met his shyly. She stood and clutched the container. "Thank you for lunch, Wyatt. It was very nice."

"So polite again." He picked up the napkin she'd written on. "Don't go away thinking I don't intend to use this. Just because I haven't pinned you down to dinner yet doesn't mean I won't."

She looked up to the sky, shaking her head a little helplessly. "I can't imagine why you'd want to pin me down for anything."

He couldn't help but grin at that. "Now there's an interesting thought," he murmured and watched the color rise up her face when she realized what he meant.

She lifted her wrist abruptly. "Look at the time. I'm late. Thanks again for the salad." She whirled on the heel of her sensible white tennis shoes and hurried away.

Wyatt laughed softly, watching the sway of her hips and the way her long ponytail swished back and forth. He *would* be calling on her again.

Sooner or later, she'd learn that he always meant what he said.

"Good grief," Felicity breathed as she peered at the computer screen in front of her. "Wyatt's even dated one of the winners of a Georgia beauty pageant." She looked over her shoulder toward Sarah-Jane where she was sitting on the couch with her own laptop, studying the knitting pattern she was designing. "Listen to this. 'Vice president and financial whiz kid of JMF Financial, Wyatt Fortune, escorts Georgianna Boudreaux to the red carpet premiere of *Texas Made,*'" she quoted. "Hey. That's that movie with the actress you made the crocheted bikini for." She studied the photo on her screen. "I think Georgianna Boudreaux's the one who had to give up her crown when nude pictures of her hit the internet."

"Great," Sarah-Jane muttered. "From beauty pageant winners to *me*." She made a mark on the pattern, expanding the grid. She wanted her "River Walk Lights" design to encompass the entire sweater and so far, she wasn't satisfied with her progress.

Probably because every time she thought about that night on the River Walk, she thought about Wyatt.

Basically, every time she thought about anything, she thought about Wyatt.

Since their lunch that afternoon, he now knew the truth about her foolish deception. But even though her conscience was clear, it hadn't stopped her from worrying at the thought of him like an itch she couldn't reach. "Wyatt needs to go back to Georgia, obviously."

"Why *obviously*?"

Sarah-Jane exhaled and gave her friend a look. "Red Rock has to be boring for him. Why else bother with me?"

"From everything I've been reading about him on the internet, it doesn't sound like he'd do anything out of boredom. If he doesn't want to stay in Red Rock, why would he?"

Sarah-Jane lifted her shoulder, trying in vain to focus on her computerized pattern. "Who knows? He hasn't talked much about himself." *Buy-it Wyatt. He told you that.*

She gave up on the pattern and went over to stand behind Felicity. She peered at the photograph on the computer screen. "That's him all right."

From the gleaming dark blond hair to the brilliantly blue, level gaze, the wry quirk of his perfectly shaped lips, and the quarterback's build, it was Wyatt Fortune. And the renounced beauty queen beside him was as different from Sarah-Jane as up was from down.

She quickly returned to the couch, but the image was burned on her mind.

Not that she needed more proof that Wyatt was ridiculously out of her league. She already *knew* that, thank you very much.

She poked at the computer keys only to close the pattern, changes entirely unsaved. She set aside the laptop, stood up and feigned a stretch. It was barely ten o'clock and she'd been home from her beginning knitting class for an hour. "I'm going to bed."

"To dream about having outrageous sex with Wyatt Fortune?"

"No," Sarah-Jane denied witheringly, but Felicity just continued grinning wickedly. "For a staunch virgin, you're awfully preoccupied with sex," she pointed out.

Felicity's expression didn't change one bit. "Just because I'm determined to wait for the right man—"

"—a marrying man, you mean—"

"Darned tootin'," her friend agreed without hesitation. "Doesn't mean I never think about *it*." She pointed at Sarah-Jane. "And don't think I don't know you're trying to veer this discussion away from yourself."

"What discussion?" Sarah-Jane tossed a decorative pillow she'd knit in True Confections' aqua at her friend's head and made for the stairway.

Felicity caught the pillow midair. "He *is* going to call you," she called after Sarah-Jane. "I can feel it in my bones. And you're going to go out with him again if it's the last thing I do!"

Sarah-Jane hurried up the steps, pretending not to hear.

She'd been the amusement of one male already once in her life. Admittedly, that humiliating experience had been nearly ten years ago. But once was more than enough.

If—and a larger if, she couldn't imagine—Wyatt did seek her out again, she would resist him.

She just wasn't exactly sure how she'd make herself accomplish it.

* * *

"Earth to Wyatt Fortune."

Wyatt looked at his little sister, who was watching him with arched eyebrows. "Did you say something?"

Her lips compressed and she shared a look with her other brothers. "I told you he wasn't listening."

They were at Red, where their sister had come to meet them for lunch. Truthfully, Wyatt *hadn't* been listening to the conversation going on around him. He'd been thinking about his lunch with Sarah-Jane the day before. "I'm listening now," he said.

She rolled her eyes. "I just said that I can show you around the area if you're really serious about looking for a place to live."

"We're serious," Asher said. He tousled Jace's hair. The little boy was sitting on a booster chair between his dad and Wyatt. "Aren't we, Jace?"

The boy nodded. "I wanna yard *this* big." He threw his arms wide, narrowly missing the glass of milk Wyatt hastily grabbed out of the way. "So my horse has lotsa room." He nodded emphatically as if by saying the words, they were magically true. "Right, Daddy?"

"We'll see, sport. Drink your milk." He waved a finger at the milk glass and Wyatt moved it back within reach of the boy.

Jace's lip poked out. "I *wan'* a horse."

Victoria leaned over the table, smiling into Jace's face. "Remember Trixie? Uncle Garrett says she's going to have her puppies any day. Maybe your daddy will let you come spend the night with us again after they're born."

"Can I have a puppy?" Jace was distracted all right, looking excitedly from his aunt to his dad.

"I don't know, Jace," Asher said, but he was giving their little sister a wry look. "We'll see."

Victoria tossed her long dark curls over her shoulder, obviously not cowed one bit. "It'll be weeks before the puppies can leave Trixie, sweetheart. But I know you'll come visit us lots and lots, so you'll be able to see them as much as you want."

Jace heaved a sigh, seemingly mollified for now. "Can I have chocolate in my milk? Please," he tacked on and Asher nodded, gesturing for the waitress.

Victoria looked back at Wyatt. "So what do you say?" She was practically bouncing with enthusiasm. "I love the idea that you're going to be living here in Red Rock. Let me help you find the perfect place." Her gaze took in the others. "What sort of property do you guys want?"

"I'm not sure I want one at all," Sawyer reminded. He elbowed Shane beside him. "Are you?"

Their eldest brother just shook his head once and continued poking at his meal. "Look at whatever you want," he finally said.

Victoria's brown gaze returned to Wyatt's. "Well?"

"I don't know," he said slowly. He'd noticed that Shane had been pretty silent and distracted for days; even more so than the rest of them. He also knew that trying to get him to open up would be as impossible as it was getting James to explain his behavior that had set all of this in motion in the first place.

He focused again on his baby sister. Sarah-Jane's hair was just as long as Victoria's, but where Vic's was glossy and dark brown, it didn't hold the red fire that Sarah-Jane's did.

"Something different than the condo I have in Atlanta," he told her as much to get his thoughts off of Sarah-Jane as anything. But as soon as he voiced the thought, it felt right. Moving to Red Rock was about making changes. Major changes.

"So, a house then." Victoria was nodding.

"With a big yard," Jace added.

"I don't want a horse," Wyatt told his nephew, laughing

a little. Or did he? Horses? Dogs? *A kid of his own with liquid brown eyes*?

The thought came out of nowhere. He shook it off like an irritating fly.

"You should," Jace was telling him seriously. He had a chocolate milk mustache. "There's nothing better than a horse."

Sawyer laughed outright at that. "And you'll probably keep thinking that, bucko, until you meet your first girl."

Asher gave Sawyer a quelling look.

"Girls are yucky," Jace said.

"Not all of 'em," Shane countered, surprising all of them.

Definitely not all of them, Wyatt agreed silently.

"I talked to Dad this morning," Shane added, changing the topic completely. He was staring down Wyatt.

Wyatt wasn't particularly surprised. That was Shane. "Did he decide to explain himself? Tell you that he's changed his mind?"

His brother's lips tightened. He shook his head once.

"Big surprise there," Wyatt muttered.

"We can't just let things go so easily, Wy."

"Why not?" Wyatt's mood darkened even more. "Just following in the old man's footsteps. He's letting go pretty da—" He saw Jace's avid expression. "Darn easily, far as I can tell. He's just not explaining his reasons why."

"Let's not talk about Daddy," Victoria begged. "I don't want to ruin a perfectly good lunch."

Too late. Wyatt pulled out his wallet and tossed enough cash on the table to cover his share of the meal. "Do your scouting and call me when you have some ideas," he told Victoria.

"Where're you going now?"

"I've got an errand to run."

"Or a woman to woo," Sawyer drawled, giving Wyatt a goading look.

Victoria's brown eyes sharpened like a cat on the hunt. "Woo? Who?" She grinned, obviously pleased with her own wit. "Anyone in particular?"

Wyatt gave Sawyer a hard look. "No."

"Yeah, right." Shane pushed aside his half-finished plate. "More like that stacked brunette who works at that sewing place."

"Knitting," Wyatt corrected automatically, only to wish he'd kept his mouth shut. *And her hair is auburn, or are you blind?*

"The Stocking Stitch?" Victoria gave Wyatt a speculative look. "Well, well, well. Maybe it's time I took up a new hobby."

Wyatt gave her a stern look. "Keep your inquisitive nose away from that shop and Sarah-Jane."

Victoria looked even more delighted. "Wyatt, you're sounding positively protective. Love once again strikes a Fortune in Red Rock. The blessing lives on."

Sawyer hooted. "Michael called that the Red Rock curse."

"You're all freaking crazy," Wyatt muttered, turning to leave.

"You won't be saying that when we hear wedding bells ringing again." Victoria's laughing voice followed him.

"They'll be ringing for someone else," Wyatt promised before he left the restaurant. He ignored the laughter that followed him.

Seeing Sarah-Jane was a lot more preferable than putting up with his siblings or thinking about anything else going on in his life, even if he couldn't seem to get the memory of her veiled in that pretty ivory wrap the night he'd taken her to the River Walk out of his head.

Chapter Six

Sarah-Jane tilted back her head, enjoying the feel of the sunlight on her face. It was a chilly afternoon in the Red Rock Community Park, but the sky was typically brilliant and the sun even more so.

She liked the lush, green park with its meandering walking trails and sturdy, rustic wood benches scattered everywhere. In the mornings before work, she often ran there. Then during her lunch break, she'd sit among the trees and watch the ducks swimming on the small man-made lake; or join the ever-changing rotation of young mothers beneath the triangular sails stretched above the playground area where their toddlers were romping; or like today, sit in the middle of a quiet stretch of emerald green grass with the sun shining down on her head.

A soft squawk had her looking down at the small birds hopping through the grass a few feet from her bench. She smiled, watching the birds, and scooped another handful of birdseed from the plastic bag she'd brought with her, and tossed a portion toward them. The hopping grew even more frenzied as the little brown creatures raced to nab a morsel before their competition could.

"What kind of birds are they?"

Startled, she felt the birdseed still in her hand slide through her fingers to her feet. Several birds bravely hopped closer, pecking up their prized seeds from right around Sarah-Jane's shoes. She hardly noticed.

She was too busy staring at Wyatt.

"I have no idea," she said faintly. "What are you doing here?"

"Looking for you." When he smiled, truly smiled, it showed in his eyes even if the smile on his lips was barely a faint curve. "I stopped by the shop," he added. "They told me where you were. Mind if I join you?"

Was he serious? Thoroughly bemused, she shook her head.

He was wearing faded blue jeans and a white button-down shirt and was holding the same leather jacket from the day before bunched in his fist with no regard whatsoever for what was probably the most expensive leather that money could buy. And when he sat down on the bench beside her, she couldn't help but inhale his masculine scent.

He smelled even better than the park on a chilly afternoon.

He angled his head, looking at the birds that had only scattered for as long as it took for him to sit down before they bounced back to resume their treasure hunt. "Looks like you have some loyal friends here."

Sarah-Jane dragged her gaze from the choppy dark gold lock falling across his forehead and looked down at the birds. "They're loyal as long as I remember to bring them something to eat." She held up the small, plastic bag that was nearly empty. "They'll be gone soon enough when the supply runs out."

"So they're greedy, too." He cupped the bottom of the bag

with one hand and reached inside with his other, his knuckles brushing against hers, and came up with a small handful. He tossed the seeds farther afield and the birds chirped and hopped, only to scatter when a larger bird swooped down on them. His lips tilted and he looked back at Sarah-Jane.

Caught staring at him, she felt her face warm. "The sun's very bright today," she said, inanely.

His smile was almost impossibly gentle and the faint lines at the corners of his eyes crinkled. "I like it." He looked back out at the grounds. "This is a nice park you've got, Sarah-Jane."

"Well." She laughed shortly. "It's a nice community park that Red Rock has, anyway."

He shook his head, his blue gaze sliding over her. "I saw the sign when I got here. But it's always going to be Sarah-Jane's park to me from now on."

The pleasure melting through her was silly. She knew it, but was helpless to stop it. All of which just made her feel like she was still the same foolish schoolgirl who'd believed every word uttered by the popular football jock who'd suddenly taken a notice in her.

She tipped the few seeds remaining in the bag on to her palm and tossed them far off to one side, toward a tiny little bird. It pounced on one of the largest of the seeds, narrowly escaping with the treat before a larger bird could snatch it away from him.

"Do you come and feed the birds every day?"

"Usually." She didn't look at him, but that didn't mean she wasn't aware of him with every cell she possessed. "Obviously not yesterday."

"The birds' loss was my gain."

She sighed a little and looked at him from the corner of her eyes. "Why do you keep saying things like that?"

"Why do you keep believing I don't mean what I say?"

She frowned, having no ready answer for that. At least no answer she cared to admit aloud.

As if he knew it, he picked up the plastic bowl sitting on the bench between them. "*Your* lunch, I assume?" He peeked under the plastic lid and tsked. "Looks like you didn't eat much of it."

"I had enough to have my fill of lettuce and cucumbers," she assured dryly.

"Surprised it's not bread so you could let your feathered friends here finish it off for you."

"Better them to have the useless carbs than me." She leaned down and picked a sunflower seed from the toe of her tennis shoe, and tossed it farther off in the grass.

"From where I'm sitting, it doesn't look like you need to be worrying about carbohydrates, useless or otherwise."

Feeling more self-conscious than ever, she tugged on the end of her ponytail, then flipped it behind her shoulder. She wasn't used to compliments, whether they were only kind lies or not. "You wouldn't have said that a few months ago, believe me."

He plucked a slice of cucumber from among the lettuce and ate it, his blue gaze on her all the while. "Why's that?"

What was it about the man's steady gaze that had every thought she possessed drooling out of her mouth? "Nothing. I've...just lost a few pounds recently." She shrugged as if the words meant nothing.

His gaze didn't waver. "I doubt that you needed to, but if you feel better about yourself, then more power to you."

She didn't know what sort of reaction—if any at all—that she'd expected, but it didn't seem to be that. "I thought I'd feel differently." She heard the words coming out of her mouth with a sort of horror. "But I look in the mirror and still see the same old me."

"I grew ten inches my senior year in high school. Until

then, the mildest description for me was scrawny. I still feel like the runt of my brothers."

"But that's ridiculous," she exclaimed. "I've seen all of you together and you're the—" She broke off before she could tell him he was the best looking of them all. Scrawny wasn't even in the dictionary of words that could describe him.

He had a slight smile on his face. "Everyone is always their own harshest critic."

"Thought you studied finance. Not human nature."

His grin flashed. "And girls. Don't forget the girls. I was finally taller than most of them."

"Even Georgianna Boudreaux?"

He raised an eyebrow. "How do you know about *her?*"

Darned tongue. "My roommate happened to mention it." She figured the words were true enough.

Wyatt managed to keep himself from grinning even more. She was curious about him. Pretending she really wasn't, but he could still see it in her eyes.

He imagined that he could see every thought she possessed in those beautiful eyes of hers. It was at once unnerving and sexy. Unnerving because it brought home so clearly the fact that she didn't possess the hardened, protective layers he was accustomed to. Despite the moments he seemed to break through it, she continued to cloak herself with wariness. But her eyes were where the wariness fell short, leaving just the vulnerability that was as sexy as it was unsettling.

"I would have been a lot taller than George if she'd ever worn regular shoes instead of those stilts she liked." He had dated the woman only a few times. She'd been interesting enough, but he'd never once looked into her eyes and felt the unfamiliar stirring he felt with Sarah-Jane. "I really do want to see you again," he said quietly. "I'd like to pick up where we left off the other night in San Antonio."

She looked away, presenting him with her profile. Her fingers worried at the empty birdseed bag.

"But if you want to start fresh, okay. If all you're ready for is to let me sit here on the park bench with you, feeding birds, then that's what I'll do."

She gave him a quick glance. "I thought you wanted to take me out to dinner." Color suffused her face and she clamped her lips closed.

He smiled and slipped the warm, fiery strands of hair that had come loose from her ponytail behind her ear. His fingers grazed her creamy cheek when he lowered his hand and he saw her pupils widen before she quickly looked away again.

"I do want to take you out for dinner." And a lot of other places. Any place. Including bed. "But I think Sarah-Jane might be more comfortable with something simpler than that. Like lunch on a park bench."

"Unlike Savannah," she murmured.

Her expressions were so open, it was like reading a book. "I don't know what your deal is with the name, but the same woman I went to San Antonio with is the same woman I'm looking at now."

Her lashes lifted and the longing in them was almost more than he could withstand. "You really think that?"

"I know that," he said quietly. Then, because he wasn't sure if he could sit there another second without putting his mouth on hers, he stood and backed away. "Tomorrow. Same park bench. Same park. Agreed?"

She hesitated, then nodded. Once. Twice. "Agreed," she said softly.

"Oh my God." Felicity clasped her plastic-gloved hands to her chest, smearing melted chocolate on the front of her apron. "That is *the* most romantic thing I've ever heard. He's going to meet you in the park! Just think, someday when you're celebrating your anniversary, you can tell your kids that you fell in love with their daddy on a park bench."

Sarah-Jane gaped. "It's *lunch!* Don't go imagining craziness, now." She shook her head sternly, as if she hadn't considered Wyatt's suggestion to be exactly as romantic as Felicity thought, and continued laboriously trying to replicate the perfect little "TC" swirl that her roommate left atop the dark chocolate truffles they were making. Felicity was able to complete at least five truffles for every single one of Sarah-Jane's. "Anniversary," she muttered. "You've been smelling too much chocolate, I think. It's going to your head."

"And you haven't been smelling enough." Felicity took the tray of truffles that Sarah-Jane was laboring over and had them finished in a blink. "Take off your gloves and wash your hands," she ordered, carrying the tray over to the counter where it joined several others. "We'll come back and box these up later." She tossed her plastic gloves in the trash and took off her apron. "Well?" She gestured when she noticed that Sarah-Jane hadn't done the same. "Come on, now. We don't have any time to waste."

Sarah-Jane was almost afraid to ask. She pulled off the thin gloves and rolled them in a ball. "For what?"

Felicity heaved a sigh and moved behind Sarah-Jane. She plucked the plastic ball of gloves out of her hand and lobbed it into the trash, then tugged the apron over her head. "Shopping," she said succinctly. "We've got maybe an hour before the shops close."

"I don't want to go shopping," Sarah-Jane protested, even as she let herself be pulled along by her determined friend. "I hate shopping."

"Too bad," Felicity said airily. "Maybe you and Wyatt won't have a wedding anniversary to celebrate someday, but tomorrow you do have a date. And it's long past time you spent a little of that money you squirrel away every paycheck on some clothes that actually *fit*."

Sarah-Jane looked down at her shirt. She was still in her "uniform" of polo shirt and khakis from The Stocking Stitch. "What's wrong with these?"

"Honestly." Felicity shook her head and physically steered Sarah-Jane toward her hybrid where it was parked in front of the candy shop. "I'll enumerate all the reasons they're wrong while you drive, starting with the fact that those polo shirts were too big for you even *before* you lost weight!"

Sarah-Jane pulled open the driver's side door but hesitated, looking at Felicity across the top of the car. "What if he doesn't show up tomorrow?"

Felicity's expression softened. "He will, Sarah-Jane."

If only she had her friend's confidence. But Sarah-Jane got in the car, anyway. "Where to?"

"Well, not the discount superstore," Felicity said wryly. "We'll start at Charlene's and work from there."

"Char—" Sarah-Jane practically choked on the name of the exclusive boutique where people the likes of Wendy Fortune shopped. "Even if I could find something that fits me there—which I doubt—I can't afford clothes from a place like that."

"Ha! Shows you what you know. Charlene, herself, was in my shop this afternoon. She told me she's having her twice-yearly sale. And I'll bet you loading and unloading the dishwasher for the next week that she *does* have something that'll fit you."

Sarah-Jane rolled her eyes. "Fine. But you're going to lose that bet."

"I don't think so." Felicity gave a superior smile.

An hour later, Felicity was right and Sarah-Jane felt hot and tired from trying on what had to have been two dozen different outfits.

But she bought several, including a dress, as well as pretty

panties and delicate-looking bras that she'd never, ever believed she could wear. The fact that she could made the ex-
orbitant price tags worthwhile. And as she and Felicity left
the store, which Charlene locked up after them, she figured
that even if Wyatt didn't show up in the park for lunch, at
least she'd have a dress to wear to her dad's birthday barbecue that would surely satisfy her mother.

The next morning, Sarah-Jane packed her lunch for work,
wondering if she ought to dare the fates and pack enough
for two. Dithering over the matter at all was embarrassing
and she was glad that Felicity had already gone off to True
Confections. She finally settled on her usual portion of salad
and chopped, fresh vegetables. But at the last minute, she ran
back inside the apartment, made a second salad and added
two apples to the bag.

It seemed fantastic to her that Wyatt would want to share
her completely boring, simple lunch, but if he *did*, she'd rather
be prepared than not.

Then, tugging the shirttail hem of the new, tailored red
blouse over the hips of her new, slim-fitting black slacks, she
hurried to The Stocking Stitch.

And then, it was a matter of focusing enough to actually
do her job, and not keep checking the time on her watch every
five minutes. But finally, after what seemed an endless morning, the hands on her watch were straight up. Noon.

Trying not to look overly anxious, she went into the office where Maria was working at the desk, and retrieved her
lunch from the small refrigerator they kept there. "I'm going
to the park," she said breezily.

Maria didn't look up from what she was doing. "You have
a nice time with your young man, niña."

Sarah-Jane hadn't uttered one word about Wyatt. "I don't
know what you mean."

Maria just gave her a look over the top of her narrow reading glasses. "You have new clothes. Your hair isn't dragged back in that ponytail for once. And you look lovely, by the way. Are you saying that's *not* because of Wyatt Fortune?"

"Felicity talked me into some new clothes," she muttered.

"Good for Felicity," Maria said mildly but she was obviously amused. She waved her hand in a brushing motion. "No, go on. When you get back from lunch, I have an appointment this afternoon."

"Oh. Well, I promise not to be late."

"Sarah-Jane." Another over-the-reading-glasses look. "I could set my watch based on your timeliness. I'm hoping you'll find you *want* to be a little late leaving the company of your suitor."

"Oh, Maria." Sarah-Jane rolled her eyes and quickly left the store before it became even more obvious to her boss just how badly she already did want Wyatt's company.

She went by foot as she always did, and had to forcibly slow her footsteps more than once. She absolutely refused to *jog* to the park. It was bad enough that she had hardly been able to sleep the night before. Or that she had kept getting out of bed to pull her new clothes out of the closet, changing her mind over and over again, whether to even wear them at all.

She realized she'd picked up her pace again when she nearly flew past the Community Park sign and slowed yet again as she turned along one of the walking paths. Her pulse was pounding, and it had nothing to do with her anxious feet. *Don't lose your cool when he's not there.*

She passed the benches by the lake area. Tugged nervously at her shirt-tail again. Plucked at the front to make sure the buttons weren't gaping over her breasts. But the shirt was so well fitted, there were no gapes. The almost wispy white bra beneath was completely hidden. No overblown cleavage anywhere. She felt…almost normal.

It's just lunch in the park.

She passed the playground area. Little kids were screeching and laughing.

Just a typical afternoon. No big deal.

Then her pulse just seemed to stop cold. Probably because her heart had jumped straight into her throat.

Not only had Wyatt shown up, but he was already there, before her. Sitting on the bench, facing away from her. But she'd recognize the back of his head anywhere.

She felt a little dizzy. Remembered that breathing tended to help that, and drew a shaky breath. She was a grown woman. Not a schoolgirl. It was time she remembered that.

She adjusted her grip on her insulated lunch bag and walked around the bench. The cluster of birds hovering in the grass nearby flew away, but she knew they wouldn't be gone long. "You made it," she greeted, as if she'd believed all along that he would.

He pulled off his sunglasses and smiled at her, right up into his eyes. Her heart skidded around all over again, making nonsense out of her "grown woman" pep talk.

"So did you." And he *did* sound surprised. "I was afraid you'd change your mind." He slid a few inches until he wasn't sitting quite in the center of the bench. "Your seat awaits."

He'd left her plenty of room to sit, but there'd be less space between them than if he'd just moved all the way to one side. Her mouth felt dry as she sat down next to him.

His thigh was only a few inches from hers.

Hers. Not Savannah's.

For a moment, she had to squelch a little spurt of hysteria. Was she turning into some sort of psychotic? Had there been a split personality lurking inside her all these years?

She banished the feeling and made a production of opening her zippered lunch bag. "Savannah" had been like playing a part in a fantasy.

Sarah-Jane was only too real. Nor did she believe in real-life fantasies.

"I hope you don't mind salad," she said brightly. "There's an apple, too." She pulled it out and held it toward him. "If you want."

"A beautiful woman offering an apple." His lips tilted. He tucked the bow of his sunglasses down the neck of his pale gray Henley shirt and she caught a glimpse of the warm tanned skin underneath. "Glad I'm not the first one to cave to temptation, because I'd have to, even if I were." His fingers brushed hers as he took the shining red apple from her.

Sarah-Jane nearly swallowed her tongue when his white teeth sank into the fruit with relish. He propped the ankle of his cowboy boot on top of the opposite knee and stretched an arm behind her on the back of the park bench. "This is the best seat in the house," he said.

She managed a nod, focusing on the returning birds. "Not too many birds hang out around the playground. Too many children making too much noise, I suppose. And over by the lake, the ducks tend to rule." She stuck her hand in her lunch bag and came out with another plastic baggie. "I brought more birdseed, too." She glanced up at him as she wedged the bag in the space between them on the bench and saw the amusement in his blue gaze.

"You look very pretty in red, Sarah-Jane," he said softly.

Her breath escaped in a whoosh. Feeling self-conscious, she plucked at the collar and looked back at the birds. But her gaze kept straying back to his face.

He needed a shave, but the blur of brown over his hard jaw only seemed to make him more mouthwatering.

He probably looks just like that when he wakes up.

The thought had her nearly squirming in her seat. "My roommate, Felicity, chose it, actually."

"Felicity has good taste."

Sarah-Jane let out a breathless laugh. "Expensive taste, when it's my savings she's spending." Which wasn't true at all. Her friend was as good at finding bargains as anyone Sarah-Jane had ever met. But even marked down by fifty percent, the clothes she'd purchased at Charlene's had not come inexpensively.

Wyatt's head was cocked slightly as he looked at her. "Is that a problem? Dipping into your savings?"

She flushed and shook her head. Only her parents had ever been interested in whether or not she was putting money away in savings. Her dad, because he was a banker. Her mom, because she figured Sarah-Jane would never find a man to support her. Not that Sarah-Jane *wanted* a man to support her. She was an MBA, for heaven's sake. She could support herself.

She realized that Wyatt was still waiting for an answer. "Not at all," she said airily. What had she ever had money to spend on, anyway? Her only vice these days was rare yarn. "What about you?" She raised her eyebrows. "What kind of work do you do in Atlanta that you can afford to leave it in order to stay in Red Rock for a while?"

"It'll be more than a while." He took another bite of the apple and heat streaked through her.

Good Lord. She was getting turned on watching him eat an *apple*. She fumbled with one of the salad containers and wrenched it open, managing to spill out several pieces of lettuce on her lap in the process.

She quickly brushed them away, pushing them back in the bottom of her lunch bag.

"Missed one."

She went still when Wyatt's hand entered her vision and plucked the piece of iceberg off the pocket that was stitched right over her breast.

He hadn't even touched her. Just the lettuce. But she still felt branded, anyway.

He flicked the lettuce off into the grass. One little bird hopped over curiously, poked around at it, then finally snatched it in his beak and flew away.

"To answer your question," he went on as if the moment had never happened, "I'm hoping to buy property in Red Rock."

Surprised, she shifted slightly, turning more toward him. "To live here?" For how long?

"Why not? Red Rock's served my sister pretty well. She loves it here." His lips tilted. "She's probably scouting places as we speak."

"But what about JMF?"

His gaze sharpened and her cheeks went hot all over again. "What do you know about JMF?"

Darn Felicity's internet snooping, anyway. It had left Sarah-Jane with far too much background information that she ought to be coming by from the source. She shrugged casually. "Nothing. I just heard somewhere that's where you worked." She couldn't help but notice the way his expression tightened, and she badly wanted to salvage the conversation. "Your father founded it or something, didn't he?"

"Yes." The word was clipped. He twisted off the stem of the apple and tossed it toward the birds before taking another bite.

Okay, so talking about *that* wasn't the way toward salvaging anything.

"What, um, what sort of place are you interested in buying?" she asked quickly. He'd brought up the matter himself; surely it was a safe topic. "A house? A condo?" He didn't seem interested in the salad—not that she could blame him—so she poked her fork into a chunk of tomato. "I'd like to buy a house someday." She knew she was chattering, but plowed on, anyway. "That's what the savings is all about. So I'll have a decent down payment. Another six months—maybe a year—and I'll probably start looking."

"What about Felicity? Tired of having a roommate?"

"Not at all." She realized the tomato was still on her fork and quickly popped it in her mouth, swallowing before continuing. "I love living with her. From the moment we met, she's been my best friend. If I do buy, it'll have to have room for her."

"What if there's a man in the picture?"

She shivered, and blamed it on the wind that had sprung up out of nowhere. "So far, Felicity's boyfriends have come and gone." Too many were more interested in a friends-with-benefits status than an actual commitment. "If that changes—*when* it changes—I'll be happy for her, of course."

"And you?"

"And me what?"

"What if there's a man in the picture for *you?*" His deep voice was the soul of patience.

She was forgetting how to breathe again. But for once she didn't shy away from his oh-so-direct gaze. "I guess I'll have to wait and see, won't I?"

He smiled slightly. Tilted his head just a little, as if acknowledging the point. "I guess we will."

We.

She swallowed. Hard.

He seemed to take pity on her then, finishing his apple, before changing the subject entirely. "Getting windy out." He looked up at the clouds skidding across the blue sky. "Wonder if we'll get a storm out of this. Are you warm enough?"

"I'm fine." She was more than warm enough, from the inside out, just from sitting so close to him. "I hope it rains at least. We could use the water. As long as we don't have a repeat of the tornado that came through here last year." She shuddered. "That was terrible. It struck right out at the airport and a few people died."

"I know. My sister was caught in it."

She nodded. "I remember. She'd been out here for Wendy's wedding, right?"

He gave her a curious look. "Yeah."

She smiled. "We hear everything sooner or later at The Stocking Stitch."

"Then you probably know she was heading home to Atlanta. Trying to head home, anyway. There were a lot of family members at the airport that day. Fortunately, everyone who was injured has recovered."

She laughed softly. "Or gotten married."

Wyatt nodded wryly. "Or that. Where were you?"

"Miles and miles away. I was at my parents' house in Houston for New Year's."

"But you didn't go there this year, obviously."

"They were traveling over the holidays." She felt a grin slip out. "I'm hoping they do that every year." She laughed softly and shook her head. "Isn't that a terrible thing to say?"

"Not everyone gets along with their parents."

She almost—*almost*—asked if he got along with his, but caught herself. She didn't want to chance asking something so personal that he got that tight look around his eyes again. "Well," she said instead, "holidays with my mother are an... experience."

"You can't just leave it there. You've got me curious, now." He angled sideways and his knee brushed against hers. And stayed there.

What would she do if he ever touched her? Really touched her? Or really kissed her? Not on her cheek or her forehead or her knuckles.

Imagining it almost made her feel dizzy. "Curious about what?"

He smiled slowly. She felt almost certain that he knew the effect he had on her, and was using it deliberately. "What kind of experience is it spending holidays with your mother?"

She tried looking away from his eyes, but couldn't seem to accomplish it. "Where to start," she said faintly and with far more humor than she usually felt. "I think I told you before that I don't have any brothers or sisters." He nodded and she was glad he didn't have to remind her that she'd been in her Savannah-mode when that conversation had taken place. "Anyway, I'm the daughter she never wanted. Too fat. Too klutzy."

"You're neither fat nor a klutz." He leaned closer until his mouth was close to her ear. She had to physically hold herself still, or she might have melted into the park bench. "Sarah-Jane, trust me on this. Whether you can recognize it or not, you have a seriously rockin' body."

Then he sat back and, ignoring the stunned, mute way she was sitting there like a lump, opened the bag of birdseed and tossed a handful out into the grass. "So. Same time tomorrow?"

All she could do was nod.

Chapter Seven

Wyatt met Sarah-Jane at the park the next day as prom-ised. This time, though, she beat him to their bench. Instead of the salad she'd brought the day before, she had a plastic-wrapped sandwich waiting for him. That, and a large, shin-ing red apple.

He'd never before had reason to think an apple was erotic, but since the day before when she'd offered him one on the palm of her hand, he'd had to revise that particular opinion.

She'd asked if he'd wanted it.

Damn near all he could think when he was near her was *want*.

In honor of the weather that had remained cloudy and windy, albeit rainless, she wore blue jeans and a thick green sweater that reached all the way down her thighs and made her brown eyes take on yet another intriguing cast. "Fire your thief yet?" he greeted.

She angled her chin, but didn't look away from him. "Not

yet." She picked up the sandwich that had been sitting beside her and gestured. "Your seat awaits."

He grinned and sat.

"You're missing out on considerably finer food at your hotel, you know." She handed him the sandwich. "Probably just about anywhere else in town, for that matter."

"If you want to go with me, we can go just about anywhere else in town."

Her cheeks went pink and her lashes swept down. He tried to remember the last time he'd spent so much time trying to…what? Get a woman into bed? He wasn't going to kid himself into thinking that's not where he wanted her. But it wasn't the only thing he wanted of her. He liked her company. Liked the humor that peeked out at him. Liked her intelligence and her heart.

Which left what to describe what he was doing with Sarah-Jane?

Wooing.

God help him.

He shoved aside the foolish notion and opened up the sandwich only to realize she had her same, usual container of undressed rabbit food. "Still no useless carbs for you, I see."

"Just for you. But I added plenty of sliced turkey breast to make up for it." She reached in her lunch container and pulled out a small, aqua-colored box. "Plus I brought you a treat." She tipped up the lid so he could see four fat truffles snuggled inside. The gaze she shot him was full of sparkle. "Make your mouth water?"

Hell yeah, his mouth was watering. But not because of the chocolate. "Looks good," he managed, and bit into the turkey sandwich. It was huge, as if she were trying to make up for the plain salad from the day before. He wanted to tell her that it didn't matter what she brought to eat for her lunch.

He was there for her.

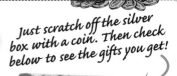
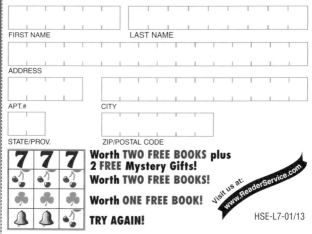

If offer card is missing, write to: Harlequin Reader Service, P.O. Box 1867, Buffalo NY 14240-1867 or visit www.ReaderService.com

HSE-3-L1-01/13

BUSINESS REPLY MAIL

FIRST-CLASS MAIL   PERMIT NO. 717   BUFFALO, NY

POSTAGE WILL BE PAID BY ADDRESSEE

HARLEQUIN READER SERVICE

PO BOX 1867

BUFFALO NY 14240-9952

NO POSTAGE
NECESSARY
IF MAILED
IN THE
UNITED STATES

Not for food.

"You sure you don't want some of this?"

She shook her head. "I've got turkey in my salad. Besides, if I ever were going to have a sandwich, I'd go whole hog and have peanut butter and jelly." Her lips twitched before she closed her mouth around a piece of tomato. The tomato had looked considerably less succulent than he was guessing her lips would be.

"I haven't had PB&J since I was a kid," he murmured. "It was always my favorite." And he'd usually had to trade whatever the cook had sent with him for lunch with another kid just to get it.

"Well," she suddenly looked shy again, "if you want to come back sometime next week, I could probably come up with one for you."

"What if I don't want to wait until next week?"

Her pupils dilated. But then a cloud passed through her gaze and she frowned, shaking her head. "I can't do anything this weekend. I'll be in Houston. It's my father's fifty-fifth birthday. My mother is throwing a big party."

Not only had she left her hair down again, but it framed her face with the same loose curls she'd had when he'd taken her to San Antonio. And like then, they seemed to be screaming at him to swirl through his fingers. "When do you leave?"

"Some time Saturday morning. My mother expects me around one or so." She sucked in her lower lip for a moment. "I'll be back Sunday night."

He would have to have been dead not to notice the way she'd left her lip moist and glistening. Some women would do that deliberately, but not Sarah-Jane.

It only made things harder.

Literally and figuratively.

He shifted slightly and studied the turkey sandwich. "Felicity going with you?"

She shook her head. "She's putting in a lot of extra hours at the shop. Valentine's Day is next month, and she's already gearing up for it."

He looked at her again, frowning. "So you're driving alone?"

"Mmm-hmm." She crunched on a slice of yellow pepper. "I've done it loads of times."

He wanted to ask about her car. If it ran reliably. Did she take her cell phone with her.

If she wanted company. Namely…him.

He squelched all the questions and wondered where the hell they'd come from. "What kind of surprising stuff do you knit or crochet?"

Her brows tugged together as she gave him a curious look. He almost felt his face flushing, knowing how abrupt he'd sounded. "You said I'd be surprised what all is—"

"—hand-knit," she finished. "I remember." The smile on her face turned positively mischievous. "Besides things like this?" She plucked at her sweater. "A few years ago we had a Hollywood crew filming between Red Rock and San Antonio. One of the actresses ordered a custom crocheted bikini."

Immediately, he wondered if she'd ever made herself such a bikini. "Intriguing," he drawled.

Maybe she had a glimpse into his mind because her gaze shied away and pink bloomed on her cheeks. "Felicity told me I should go into business selling them." Her tone made it plain what she thought of that. "I'd rather be in the business of selling the patterns." She grinned suddenly. "And what do you know? I *am*."

He couldn't help but chuckle. She was so obviously pleased with herself. The fact that she loved what she did was as plain as the nose on her face.

Until his father's unwelcome decision, Wyatt had felt the same way.

He tried pushing aside the thought. He'd already had his fill earlier that day of talk about JMF. Shane—despite every argument that Wyatt and his brothers could think of—had returned to Atlanta that morning. He claimed he wasn't returning to JMF as well, but Wyatt figured it was only a matter of time before he did. His brother wouldn't be able to stay away, anymore than the rest of them could.

That was the advantage of relocating all the way to Red Rock. No proximity to JMF's offices.

The other advantage was sitting on the park bench next to him, turning his guts into a knot and smelling like warm vanilla on a blustery afternoon.

"Your dad's only turning fifty-five? What's he do?"

"He's an assistant bank manager." She shook her head against a lock of hair that the breeze nudged into her eyes.

"And your mom?"

"Stay-at-home mom. Always has been, always will be." She looked down at her salad and jabbed a chunk of turkey. "She and my dad married right after he graduated from college, and she promptly quit school to become the perfect wife and hostess."

"You don't think she should have quit school?"

She shot him a look. "Why would you ask that?"

He shrugged. "Something in your voice."

"It doesn't matter whether I think that or not. What matters is what she thinks."

"And what does she think?"

Her brows tugged together for a moment. "You know," she said slowly, "I really have no idea." She squinted out at the birds. Only a few had remained, staunchly optimistic that a morsel would be forthcoming. The other dozen or so had departed for more fertile grounds around the nearby lake. "She certainly pushed me to get my college degree," she finally said.

"Maybe because she didn't get one herself."

She snorted softly. "More like because she thinks at least I'll to be able to support myself, since no man is ever likely to want to do it for me." She slid him a look. "In my mother's world, a woman only *finishes* her education if she hasn't caught a husband by then."

"Seems to be the way a lot of our parents' generation thought."

"Yeah, well—" she jabbed another chunk of meat "—it's a new generation," she muttered, and bit the meat off the fork with her perfectly even, white teeth. After she swallowed, she looked at him. His sandwich.

He quickly took another bite. It was a good sandwich, no question. He just kept getting distracted by her. "How'd you end up living in Red Rock?"

Her demeanor brightened as if a cloud had drifted beyond it. "Maria Mendoza. After I'd discovered knitting in college, I heard about her store and came to see it. I fell in love with the place. I didn't expect to fall in love with Red Rock, too, but I did. Once I finished my MBA, I knew I wanted to live here, too." She gave a wry smile. "Actually, I initially applied for a position with the Fortune Foundation."

The Fortune Foundation, Wyatt knew, had been founded in memory of one of his father's distant relatives, Ryan Fortune, when he'd died nearly ten years earlier. A number of far-flung extended family members worked at the ever-growing, philanthropic concern. "But no go?"

"Not at all. I would have had the job if I hadn't decided to go to work full-time for Maria instead." She smiled and mischief was back in her expression. "My mother had a fit."

"What about your dad?"

She shrugged. "As long as I keep putting away money into my savings on a regular basis, I don't think my dad cares much one way or the other how I've earned it." Her smiling gaze skipped over him. "Long as it's legal, of course."

With a sort of detached interest, he noticed his hand sliding through her hair, moving it away from her cheek again. "I'll jump in that cold lake over there if you've ever done anything illegal in your life."

Her gaze had gone shy again, but not shy enough to look away from him. "Well, I guess your clothes are safe enough from getting wet today." Then her chin tilted a little challengingly. "I'm sure you've never done anything illegal, either."

"I wouldn't say that, necessarily."

She gave him a skeptical look. "Okay, then what?"

"Just stupid college stuff." He grinned wryly. "Mostly involving fast cars."

She laughed. "And overflowing testosterone, no doubt."

Her hair slid through his fingers, a curl winding around his thumb. He closed his fingers and tugged gently.

Her lips parted slightly, her eyes widening as she looked up at him.

It would be so easy to kiss her.

And too damn hard to stop, he feared.

Instead, he tugged her hair again, the same way he used to tug on Victoria's, and let her loose.

Sarah-Jane blinked, trying to bring her scrambled thoughts back together again. Had she imagined that he was going to kiss her?

"Do you have your cell phone with you?"

Evidently, she *had* imagined it.

Foolish, Sarah-Jane. She never learned.

"Yes. I have my cell phone. Why?"

"Can I see it?"

She didn't know what to make of the man, but slid the small phone out of a pocket on the side of her insulated lunch bag. He took it from her and began tapping on it. "I want you to call me when you get back from your parents' house." He finished tapping and handed back the phone. "My private number's saved in there now."

Her thumb roved over the face of the phone. She eyed him, but he was already sinking his strong teeth into the sandwich again.

"It'll be late Sunday night before I get back."

"Doesn't matter how late. Otherwise I'll worry about you driving all that way on your own."

Okay. It wasn't a kiss. But the fact that he'd worry about her was pretty darn bemusing. "What, um, what are you doing this weekend?" One portion of her mind wished that he'd tell her he wanted to come with her to Houston. The rest of her logic flatly squashed the wish. Even if he did suggest it—which he wouldn't—she didn't particularly want him witnessing the way she really was. And if he saw her with her parents—one of whom was never satisfied, and the other who hardly noticed her at all—he would definitely be seeing Sarah-Jane as she really was.

He polished off the sandwich with one more bite, then wiped his mouth and hands on one of the paper napkins she'd brought. "Victoria has a property she wants us to see. We'll probably spend some time out at her place, too. Give Jace a chance to race around outside and play with the dogs."

She knew Jace was his nephew. He'd mentioned him a few times the night they'd gone to San Antonio. "Are his parents divorced?"

Wyatt nodded. "Lynn's out of the picture. Ash raises him on his own." He picked up the bag of birdseed, weighing it in the palm of his long-fingered hand. "Red Rock will be good for them, too. Change of scene." He tossed a small handful of seeds out and birds dove squawking and screeching from every corner. "Jace insists he wants a horse."

She believed it was the most he'd ever spoken about anyone in his family. Holding the pleasure close, she curtailed the impulse to ask if he wanted children of his own someday, and smiled instead. "Doesn't every child want a horse? I certainly did."

"Did you get one?"

She made a rueful face. "I couldn't even get a dog or a cat."

"You had *no* pets?" He frowned hard.

It was a good thing her hands were occupied holding her salad on her lap or she would have wanted to smooth away that frown with her fingertip. "I had a goldfish once." She smiled into his face. "Won it at the state fair, tossing nickels onto a tower of glass dishes. My dad took me there once when I was in high school. It was the only time he'd ever done anything like that." She liked to believe that it was because he'd been trying to cheer her up after the humiliating prom incident—which he'd had no way of knowing just how humiliating.

Now, instead of frowning, Wyatt looked indulgent. "What else did you do in high school?"

"Played clarinet—badly—in the band." She shrugged, excruciatingly aware that his hand behind her on the bench had strayed to her hair again. "Studied a lot. You know. Usual stuff." Usual stuff for the shyest girl in school, at any rate. But she didn't want to talk about those years, which had been capped off by the most mortifying experience of her life. "What about you? What'd you do in high school?"

His lips twitched. "Studied a lot. You know. Usual stuff."

She huffed and rolled her eyes.

He laughed softly, stroked his fingers through her hair, and tossed the birds some more seed.

And just that simply—and that alarmingly—Sarah-Jane realized how easily she could love this man.

The realization didn't diminish at all over the next twenty

minutes, until her lunch break was at an end and Wyatt insisted on walking her back to the knitting shop.

"Remember," he prompted, when they reached The Stocking Stitch. "Call me when you get back from Houston."

"I will."

He pulled open the shop door for her and she almost thought he'd accompany her inside. But he didn't. All he did was hand her back the lunch bag that he'd carried for her and tug on a lock of her hair. "Drive carefully." Then he was walking away.

Sarah-Jane stared at him through the slowly closing glass door of the shop.

"Ah," Maria sighed behind her. "I can see you had a perfect time, didn't you, Sarah-Jane?"

Sarah-Jane couldn't deny it. But as she watched Wyatt disappear from view, she also couldn't help but wonder how long something this perfect could possibly last.

The drive to Houston the next day took Sarah-Jane almost exactly three hours. When she turned on to the tree-filled cul de sac where she'd grown up, the street in front of her parents' house was already congested with cars. She frowned a little. There wasn't even parking available in the driveway that led up to the spacious, four bedroom ranch-style house. She wasn't late. If anything, she was a little early.

She parked at the end of the street and around the corner, but instead of carrying her overnight bag all that way, she left it locked in the car. She grabbed the gift bag holding the Houston Texans football jersey she'd gotten her dad from the backseat, and then, brushing her hands down the skirt of the new swirly dress that Felicity and Charlene had talked her into, she walked back up the street to the house.

Before she got even close to the door, she could hear the music. The Beatles, which was her father's favorite.

She couldn't help but smile a little. Her mother detested The Beatles, but evidently, even Yvette Early could bend a little when she was celebrating her husband's birthday.

Nobody gave Sarah-Jane any notice as she entered through the unlocked front door and headed straight through to the back of the house, through the kitchen, and on out to the block-fenced backyard. The party was in full swing; guests were milling about everywhere she looked. She spotted her father right off; he was standing at the grill, wearing a red-and-white-checked barbecue apron and waving a long-handled fork around as he talked with a couple of men she recognized from his bank. Racks of ribs sizzled on the grill alongside chicken legs and hot dogs and the air was redolent with the mouthwatering scents. She dropped off her gift bag on the table loaded down with gifts on her way toward him.

"Happy birthday, Dad," she greeted, stepping up behind him.

He turned and gave her his typically absent smile. "Hi, honey. Glad you made it." He accepted the hug she gave him even as he was looking over her head. "Your mom is around here somewhere."

She hid a little sigh. Aside from that one trip to the state fair that had netted her the goldfish that had lived for all of two months and his continued interest in the state of her savings account, Howard Early had never been a particularly involved parent.

He'd always been off working. Or playing golf. Or working. Or working some more.

"I'll find her," she assured him, and gave a smiling greeting to his companions. They, at least, were eyeing her with a bit of surprise that her ego found shamefully gratifying.

If it hadn't been for Charlene's and Felicity's insistence that the kaleidoscope-colored halter dress looked as if it had been made for her, she never would have had the nerve to purchase something so outrageously colorful, or that left her shoulders and arms completely bare. As it was, she was wearing a thin white cardigan with it, but considering the bright sunlight overhead, she wasn't sure if she wouldn't get too warm for it. The weather had to easily be in the seventies.

She left her father to his grilling and conversation and made her way among the guests until she found her mother at the buffet tables where she was rearranging stacks of stark white plates next to a towering display of cascading fruit.

Yvette spotted Sarah-Jane as she was crossing the lawn, and she straightened up from her task, propping her hands on her hips. "It's about time you got here," she greeted, looking cross. "Your father was beginning to wonder if you'd forgotten all about his birthday."

Sarah-Jane sighed inwardly and gave her mother a kiss on the cheek. As far as she could tell, her father typically hadn't seemed bothered by her presence one way or another. It was her mother who was the one with her nylons in a knot. "Of course I didn't forget."

She also could have pointed out that she was actually a few minutes earlier than the time Yvette had given, but didn't. Adding to the aggravation on her mother's face wasn't anything she relished doing. "You look very pretty, Mom." And her mother did, wearing a buttery yellow dress that looked lovely with her still-dark hair.

Yvette made a face. "This old thing," she dismissed. "I wanted to go into the city to a proper dress boutique, but simply didn't have time." She shook her head and her shoulder length hair didn't have the nerve to budge beyond its ruthless layer of hair spray. "Doing all of this for your father hasn't been easy, you know." She gestured with the plate still in her hand for emphasis.

"I'm sure," Sarah-Jane murmured. She looked around at the festive cloths covering round tables scattered around the pristine yard and the elaborate buffet set up behind her mother. "It all looks beautiful, though."

Yvette sniffed. "It'll do." She handed the plate to Sarah-Jane. "You might as well eat something." She didn't move off as Sarah-Jane took the plate and began filling it. "Have you seen Barbara Curtis? Honestly, that woman can get away with wearing the most outrageous colors. But then I suppose when you're a size 2, anyone can."

Sarah-Jane added a few slices of cheese to the grapes on her plate. She wanted to save room for some ribs once they were off the grill. She'd run an extra five miles that morning just so she wouldn't have to feel guilty if she indulged at her dad's party. "I haven't seen her yet." She skipped over the corn bread muffins tumbling artfully from a tipped basket, and glanced around until she spotted Barbara.

The stylish woman was wearing hot pink jeans that hugged her skinny hips and an equally vivid orange sweater that was hanging precariously on the points of her tanned shoulders. Sarah-Jane looked back at her mother. "I think you look nicer."

Yvette made a face. "Don't be ridiculous, Sarah-Jane. Women like you and me can never compete with someone like Barbara. I blame my mother. It's her side of the family we take after. At least I was lucky enough to find your father." She looked at the plate in her daughter's hands and sighed dolefully. At the amount of food there, Sarah-Jane assumed. "Thank goodness he at least taught you how to save money even though you've decided to waste yourself on that little knitting shop of yours. You *are* still putting money away for the future, aren't you?"

Heaven forbid if she'd actually added coleslaw or corn bread to her plate, Sarah-Jane thought. "Yes, I'm still saving plenty of money." Aside from her shopping spree at Charlene's, of course.

"That's something I suppose." Yvette heaved a sigh. "Try not to spend too much time eating," she finally said. "There's plenty to do in the kitchen if you want to make yourself useful." She twitched at her skirt and headed off across the grass, calling gaily to a couple who'd just entered through the side gate.

Ignoring the pain that had formed in the center of her forehead, Sarah-Jane found a seat at one of the tables with the neighbors who lived across the street. They greeted her cheerfully and after a few minutes visiting with them, she threw away her plate, told her dad that people were anxious to get at his grilled masterpieces, and headed into the kitchen. Her mother's snide comment aside, she really was happier there being useful rather than trying to be a social butterfly she wasn't.

And in the kitchen is pretty much where she stayed—making trays, cleaning trays, reloading trays—until several hours later, she could see through the windows over the sink that the party was wrapping up.

"Hey there, Sarah-Jane." Martin, her father's "young" associate at the bank and the bad kisser, came into the kitchen while she was wrapping up the leftovers. His smile was practically a leer as he leaned against the counter next to where she was working. Sarah-Jane barely gave him a glance. "Hey, Martin." She couldn't for the life of her understand why her mother had bothered to serve fancy little finger sandwiches when there'd been plenty of other things to choose from. But then, Sarah-Jane wasn't the cul de sac's version of Martha Stewart, either.

Martin was still standing there. "Can I get you something?" she asked.

"Sure." He reached out and dragged his finger down her arm. "You're looking good, Sarah-Jane. Real good. What have you done to yourself?"

She pointedly moved out of his reach, wondering how many beers he'd consumed. He had one can clutched in his stubby-fingered hand. "Do you want a finger sandwich?" She picked up the plastic container she'd been stacking them in and held it between them.

He didn't give the sandwich points so much as a glance. "Why don't we get out of here? Go somewhere we can be alone?"

She barely controlled a shudder of distaste. "Like your place? Won't your mother be there?"

He blinked. "I have my own room. She'll leave us alone."

The man was simply oblivious. "It's my father's birthday, Martin," she said patiently. "I'm not going anywhere." Certainly not with him.

She tried to move past him toward the kitchen door, but he stepped in her way, wearing a sulky pout that only children who were a fraction of his age could get away with. On him it looked simply ridiculous.

"You're not getting any younger, Sarah-Jane. Don't you think it's time you took off the clamp holding your knees together and got yourself a boyfriend?"

Ugh. "I have a boyfriend," she said and felt no compunction whatsoever with the exaggeration. Wyatt wasn't her boyfriend. Not even close, considering he hadn't even kissed her, much less given the slightest attention to the state of the knees she'd kept closed since the humiliating high school prom debacle. But she'd like to think he was something of a friend. And he was certainly male.

And if he didn't like a situation, he just said so, instead of wearing a ridiculous, petulant pout.

"A *boyfriend!*" Yvette pushed at Martin from the opposite side and he stumbled forward toward Sarah-Jane, who pivoted out of the way on the soles of her wedgey sandals. "You didn't tell me you had a boyfriend, Sarah-Jane."

On the heels of Yvette was Sarah-Jane's father, and she could see his surprised expression, too.

She wanted to pull the apron she'd wrapped around herself to protect her pretty dress right over her head.

"Who is he?" her mother demanded, hands on her hips, staring at Sarah-Jane as if she recognized her claim for exactly the falsehood that it was.

"Wyatt Fortune," she said calmly, and idly pondered the fact that all of her untruths seemed to be related to him. "Wyatt Fortune is my boyfriend."

"Fortune?" Yvette's voice rose an octave. "Not one of *the* Fortunes."

Maybe later Sarah-Jane would be ashamed of the delight she took in the stupefied expressions facing her—particularly her mother's. "Yes, Mother. One of *those* Fortunes."

But all she could do now was enjoy the moment.

Chapter Seven

Felicity was rolling on the couch, peals of laughter rolling out of her mouth. "Classic," she managed breathlessly. "I wish I could have seen your mother's expression!"

Sarah-Jane grimaced a little and moved her overnight bag from the chair where she'd dumped it to the floor so she could sit down in its place. She still had a headache, but it had lessened considerably once she'd spoken her piece and left Houston to come back home to Red Rock where she belonged. She hadn't even spent the night there, but had driven straight back.

She and Felicity had arrived at practically the same time, since her friend had put in a mammoth work session at True Confections.

"I shouldn't have told her he was my boyfriend, though. It wasn't true."

"Too bad. He's a man. He's a friend. And it stumped your mother, which is entirely worth a little exaggeration. If it even *is* an exaggeration."

"Of course it is!"

Felicity sighed noisily, but didn't argue. She sat up and rubbed her hands together. "Tell me exactly what you said to her."

Sarah-Jane lifted her eyebrows. "It's a little alarming how much delight you're taking in this."

Felicity waved her hand, dismissively. "I'm taking delight in the fact that you stood up to your mother for the first time in your life!"

And how shocked Yvette had been, too, Sarah-Jane thought. "I didn't exactly stand up to her. While she was still shocked that *I* was seeing a *Fortune,* I just told her that I wished she was happier with my life."

"And…?" Felicity's eyes were wide.

"And…that I wished she was happier with hers."

"And what'd she say?"

Sarah-Jane shook her head. "Not a single thing. She just stared at me as if she'd never seen me before."

Felicity clapped her hands together once. "And that's exactly what she needed to do. See you with fresh eyes!"

Sarah-Jane pinched the bridge of her nose. "Still, I probably should have stayed the night there."

"Why? Did you want to? Do you think it would have mattered to your dad?"

"No. And no, again." Her father had a regular golf date every weekend. Nothing, not even the fact that his daughter was visiting, would get in the way of it.

"So, I repeat, why?"

"Because…" She thought for a minute, and couldn't come up with a single, good reason. "I still feel guilty."

Felicity's expression sobered. She leaned over and grabbed Sarah-Jane's hands. "Sarah-Jane, you are one of the kindest, most loyal people I've ever known. For years I've listened to the way your mother has cut you down and your dad has either not noticed, or not cared enough to stop her. You've continued being a better daughter than they deserve. You're a grown woman and you spoke your mind for once. Don't go backtracking on that by feeling some misguided sense of guilt."

"But—"

"Don't," she cut her off. Then she pointed toward the doorway leading to the kitchen. "Something was waiting for you on the doorstep when I got home from the shop tonight."

Sarah-Jane looked over and saw a small cardboard box sitting on the kitchen table. "What is it?"

Felicity lifted her shoulders. "You tell me. It has your name on it."

She pushed out of the chair and went over to the table, studying the box. It had no mailing labels or stamps.

There was nothing to indicate the box was from Wyatt. Nothing except the squiggle of excitement shimmying through her belly and her name written in slashing, bold letters across the top of the sealed box. But she'd seen Wyatt scrawl his signature more than once. And she recognized it now.

"Here." Felicity handed her the kitchen shears. "Open it."

Sarah-Jane sliced open the tape and folded open the top. Lying inside among a nest of crumpled white tissue paper was a perfect little brown bird.

She felt her heart blooming against the inside of her chest as she slowly lifted the bird from the paper. It was small enough to sit on the palm of her hand.

"It's a candle," Felicity whispered almost reverently. She touched her fingertip to the small wick that Sarah-Jane hadn't even noticed.

Sarah-Jane could only nod. Her throat had closed up tight and her legs had gone so weak that she pulled out one of the chairs and plopped down on it. She picked up the plain white folded card that had been placed beneath the bird and opened it.

Saw this and it reminded me of the birds in Sarah-Jane's park. —W

Felicity read the card over her shoulder. "If you don't fall in love with him," she breathed, "would you mind terribly if I did?"

Too late, Sarah-Jane thought. She was afraid Felicity was much too late.

"You have to call him," Felicity said suddenly.

Alarm streaked through her. "It's nearly midnight."

"So?"

Sarah-Jane shook her head with a mile more decisiveness than she felt. "He's not expecting me back until tomorrow night." *But you did promise to call him when you returned,* a sly voice inside her head reminded. "He's not going to care if I wait until tomorrow."

Felicity pointedly stroked her finger over the inquisitive angle of the little bird's head. "Oh, really? Want to talk about how he's just a friend?"

Sarah-Jane folded her fingers gently around the beautifully detailed wax candle and pushed out of the chair. "Oh, fine," she huffed. But it was an act.

Felicity knew it.

Sarah-Jane knew it.

Even the little wax bird probably knew it.

"I'll call him upstairs." She headed through the living room again, latching her free hand through the strap of her overnighter along the way.

"I won't bother asking you to give him my regards." Felicity's laughing voice followed her. "Somehow, I think you'll fill the time with more interesting things to talk about."

Sarah-Jane quickly closed herself in her bedroom, closing off whatever else Felicity could say.

Something was churning inside her and she sank down

onto the foot of her knit-bedspread-covered bed, staring down at the sweet little bird cradled in her hand. *Oh, Wyatt. What are you doing to me?*

There was no answer. Not from the bird, at any rate, and eventually, Sarah-Jane toed off the pretty high-heeled wedgies that she'd worn with her dress and pulled her cell phone out of her purse.

Before she could lose her nerve, she found his number and quickly hit the button.

Despite the late hour, he answered on the second ring. "Sarah-Jane? Is everything okay?"

Just the sound of his deep voice in her ear made her feel warm inside. "Everything's fine. Thank you for the bird." Her thumb ran over the candle, feeling the ridges of each feather carved into the wax.

He was silent for a moment. "You're back early, I take it?"

"Yes."

"Something go wrong?"

She almost laughed, but there was a sudden burning deep behind her eyes. She could go her whole life happy without him ever knowing how little her own mother thought of her. "Nothing out of the ordinary." She cleared her throat softly. "I just decided to come back early."

He was silent for a moment and when he spoke his voice seemed to have become even deeper. "Then I can see you tomorrow."

She tucked the phone between her cheek and shoulder and swiped her cheeks, nodding. Realized he couldn't see that. "You could," she said huskily.

"Have I made it past your guard enough that I can pick you up at your apartment?"

She smiled weakly. Heaven help her if he ever learned she had no guard against him at all. "Yes."

"Ten o'clock?"

"Sure."

"Wear comfortable jeans."

"Okay, but what—"

"Good night, Sarah-Jane." He hesitated a moment. "I'm glad you like the bird."

She heard a click and her phone went silent.

Dropping the phone onto the bed beside her, she clasped the bird against her chest and fell back on the bed, exhaling shakily. But after a moment, she set the bird aside and scrambled to her feet, racing down the hall to find Felicity standing at the sink in the bathroom, a toothbrush in her mouth.

"He's picking me up here at ten in the morning!"

Felicity gave her a foamy grin. "Why 'r you s' panicked?" she managed around the toothbrush.

"Because he's picking me up at ten in the morning," she repeated as if it were obvious.

Felicity held up one finger, turned and rinsed out her mouth, then patted it dry with a towel before looking back at Sarah-Jane. "What are you guys gonna do?"

"I have no idea!" Sarah-Jane knew she looked wild-eyed. She could see her reflection in the bathroom mirror. "He just said to wear comfortable jeans. So what do I do?"

Felicity's grin widened. "Wear comfortable jeans," she suggested.

Sarah-Jane tossed up her hands and whirled on her bare foot, heading back to her room. "Fat lot of help you are."

"Let me elaborate, then." Felicity's laughing voice sounded positively delighted as she followed her. "Wear the jeans you bought from Charlene. They're the only pair in your closet that aren't baggy on you. And before you argue, comfortable doesn't mean baggy. Those jeans from Charlene's are comfortable, aren't they?"

Sarah-Jane nodded. They were perfectly comfortable. "But my old jeans are—"

Felicity spoke over her, cutting her off without mercy. "Ugly. And wear the blue sweater I gave you for Christmas."

"But that one makes my boobs look—"

"—phenomenal," Felicity interrupted. She plucked at her nightshirt. "It's the kind of sweater that could make girls like me feel positively inadequate."

"There's nothing inadequate about you in the least!"

"I said *could*." Felicity grinned. She crossed to Sarah-Jane's closet and threw open the door to push through the hangers. She pulled out three other tops and hung them on the doorknob. "Those'd work equally well. Except for your Stocking Stitch polos that I figure you'll never part with and the stuff you bought the other day, everything else in there ought to be donated as far as I'm concerned. And when Wyatt gives you a compliment—and he will—just bat your eyes and say *thank you*." She turned to leave the bedroom, but stopped when she reached the doorway. "And one last thing."

Sarah-Jane looked from the closet to her friend. "What?"

Felicity smiled wickedly. "Be sure whatever you're wearing underneath is something you don't mind being seen."

"Felicity!"

Her friend just laughed and disappeared from the doorway.

She wore jeans. And the blue sweater.

And she left her hair down just because when she pulled it in front of her shoulders it provided sort of a curtain over the clinging cashmere knit.

And she was glad that Felicity had gone to work at the shop earlier, so she wouldn't be a witness to Sarah-Jane's nervousness that just kept building until she heard a knock on the front door at ten o'clock on the dot. She exhaled hard and crossed the living room, rubbing her damp palms down the seat of her jeans before pulling open the door.

All of the nervous tension inside her turned to one big bowl of quivering goo at the sight of him. He was wearing jeans and an untucked blue-and-white plaid shirt with the sleeves rolled up his sinewy forearms, over a plain white T-shirt. And he had on a cowboy hat that looked as if it had taken as much wear as his leather boots.

If she were a brave woman, she'd just wrap her hands around the lapels of that loose shirt and yank him toward her. Instead, she wrapped her hand around the doorknob next to her and tried not to make a complete fool out of herself. "You're very prompt."

He was wearing that crooked grin that never failed to charm her. "You're very beautiful."

Heat spread from her cheeks down to her toes, stopping to fill all the points in between. Remembering Felicity's words, she managed a shaky smile. "Thank you."

His grin widened a little as his gaze travelled down to her toes. "Do you have boots?"

"Um, yeah." Was she not dressed up enough, after all? "The ones I wore when we went to San Antonio. Do I need to change?"

"Those had high heels. And no. Don't change." His gaze roved over her again, giving that heat coursing through her no chance to cool. "Definitely, do not change. Any other boots?"

"No. Sorry."

He thumbed his hat back an inch and his eyes crinkled. "Sarah-Jane, you are the furthest thing from sorry that I have ever seen."

There was nothing but warmth in his gaze and for once in her life, she didn't feel like slouching her shoulders in a futile attempt to minimize her plump breasts. "That goes likewise," she said a little breathlessly.

His smile deepened a little. "You ready to go? We'll be gone all day."

All day. Her breath went short just thinking about spending an entire day with him. "What're we doing?"

"You'll see." He stepped back, giving her room on the landing when she stepped through the door and pulled it closed to lock it. Then he touched his fingers to the small of her back and started for the parking lot. "It's a surprise."

Logically, she knew her tennis shoes had to be in contact with terra firma as they walked to the parking lot, but it seemed more like they were floating a few inches above ground. Instead of leading her to his rental car, though, he headed toward a huge, black pickup truck.

"If I'm gonna be a Texan, figure I ought to drive the part," he said when she gave him a questioning look.

She couldn't help but laugh. "Wyatt, I'm a native Texan and I drive a tiny little hybrid sedan." She looked at the truck that appeared to have been designed on steroids. "This is just a big ole toy for a man with money to burn, far as I can tell."

He gave a grunting laugh. "Strangely enough, that's pretty much what my mother said when I told her I'd bought a truck." He opened the door for her and waited until she'd stepped up on the running board and hitched herself on to the luxurious leather seat before letting go of her arm and closing the door.

Sarah-Jane hauled in a hasty breath and let it out noisily while he rounded the front of the truck. When he got in beside her, the truck no longer seemed overwhelmingly big. It obviously fit him so much more comfortably than the rental car. Even a very luxurious rental car.

His blue gaze landed on her face. "Everything good?"

How could it not be? "Mmm-hmm." She concentrated on fastening the safety belt so as not to start babbling. "So when are you going to tell me what we're doing?"

He laughed softly. "Bugging you, is it?"

She shot him a look. "Well, frankly. Yes."

His eyes sparkled wickedly. "Good." He drove out of the

lot, handling the truck with enviable ease, and soon they were heading through the middle of Red Rock. She still couldn't figure out his plan, even when he pulled into a parking spot in front of the string of shops where Charlene's was located. "Come on." With the push of a button he released her safety belt and then his own. "Got a stop to make first."

She looked out at the shops. Just seeing the sign for Charlene's reminded her all too well what she'd chosen to wear for the day. On the outside and underneath. When Wyatt took her hand and tugged her directly toward Charlene's, she wondered rather hysterically if he was able to read her mind.

But instead of Charlene's, he turned into the Western wear shop directly next door. They were greeted immediately by a middle-aged man who seemed to be the only one tending the place. "How can I help you?"

"Boots," Wyatt said. He was still holding her hand and when the clerk led them toward the back of the store, Wyatt pulled her along with him.

"We have a wide array," the clerk said, waving his arm to encompass the entire wall that held what seemed to be a hundred styles of cowboy boots. "A very fine selection for men and women." He gestured for each. "Is there anything in particular I can help you find?"

Wyatt finally let go of her hand as he headed toward a particular display of boots that was set off from all the rest. "Castletons," he murmured. "These should do."

She realized with a start that he wasn't looking at men's boots, but at women's. "Um, Wyatt?" She hurried up behind him, keeping her voice low. "Castletons are probably the most expensive boots in this place." She could pay both halves of her and Felicity's rent for several months for what she suspected was the average price of a Castleton boot. "I can't afford—"

"You don't need to afford 'em. I can." He plucked a tall

black boot with intricate turquoise stitching spreading from the toe on up to the leather shaft from the very top of the display. "Man with money to burn, remember?" He held up the boot for the clerk to see. "Are these stocked or a custom order?"

"Custom, sir."

Wyatt made a "hmming" little sound that she found distinctly alarming. Then he suddenly turned toward her. "What size shoe do you wear?"

It wasn't so much the size of her shoe that she was worried about, but fitting her calf into that tall of a boot. She'd long ago given up on ever finding a tall pair of boots that fit. The dress boots she'd worn that night in San Antonio had been much shorter and forgiving of her calves than the cowboy boot he was holding up. "I usually wear a seven and a half," she said. "But—"

Wyatt looked at the clerk again. "What size is this one?"

"It's an eight, sir, but it is a sample only."

"Do you have the mate?"

"Of course."

Wyatt handed the boot to Sarah-Jane. "You want to try it on just to see if it fits?"

She no more wanted to stick her leg down that beautiful, slender boot than she wanted to stick her head in a noose. "It's a sample," she reminded under her breath.

Wyatt gave her a steady look. Shifted his attention to the clerk once more. "You can get another *sample,* if this one fits and she decides she wants to take them, right?"

The clerk blinked a little. "Yes, sir. Of course."

Probably calculating his commission, Sarah-Jane thought sourly.

Obviously satisfied, Wyatt handed her the boot. "Just try it, Sarah-Jane." He waved a hand carelessly at the display. "Or one of the others if you like something else better."

Naturally, he'd selected the most beautiful boot from the lot. And as far as she could see, none of the other boots on display looked any more forgiving than this one. "It won't fit," she told him, but she carried it with her over to one of the wooden seats situated opposite a series of tall, narrow mirrors.

"Allow me to assist you," the clerk said quickly, moving to crouch in front of her as she toed off one of her tennis shoes and pulled up her pant leg.

Looking anywhere but at Wyatt, she pushed her stocking-clad foot into the boot, down, down, down.

"You can use the ear pulls to help tug," the clerk suggested.

As if that was going to help. But Sarah-Jane slid her fingers through the stitched loops on either side of the deep scalloped top, and pulled.

Her foot, ankle *and* calf slid as neatly into the boot as Cinderella's foot had fit into the glass slipper.

"A fine selection. Very fine," the clerk was telling Wyatt. "Castleton makes exceptional boots. They can rarely be matched for the quality of their materials or their construction."

Sarah-Jane was barely listening. She was busy looking at her reflection in the mirror across from her.

The boot had fit. The beautiful, slender looking boot had fit. And she could seriously imagine how Cinderella had felt.

She stood up experimentally. The angled heel was well over an inch, but she could still tell that the foot portion of the boot fit her own foot like it was a comfy, knitted bootie. "Can I try on the mate?"

The men stopped talking and looked at her. Wyatt smiled, looking ridiculously satisfied with himself, and she was pretty sure the clerk's eyes had dollar signs blinking inside them. He immediately headed through a swinging door in the corner.

"I'm only trying it on," Sarah-Jane told Wyatt sternly. "Because I'm curious what they'll both feel like. *Not* because I'm going to let you spend money on me like this." She'd seen the discreet sticker on the display where the boot had stood. Five months worth of rent, easy.

"You know, it's not polite to question the price of a gift."

She raised her eyebrows and gave him a stern look. "It's not seemly for a woman to accept a gift that is this pricey from a man."

He gave a choking laugh. *"Seemly?"*

"Proper!"

He suddenly pulled off his hat and tossed it on one of the wooden chairs as he stepped behind her and put his hands on her waist to pull her in front of him. Their reflections were directly opposite and Sarah-Jane couldn't drag her gaze free of his in the mirror as he angled his head lower until she not only could see his lips near her ear, but feel his breath as well, especially when he slid her hair behind her shoulder and tucked it behind that ear. "I could buy out the entire inventory of this place and give it to you, and still be more proper than if I were to tell you what I think of you in these jeans and this sweater."

She saw her lips part, her eyes widen and rosy color spread across her cheeks.

But mostly, oh, mostly she felt his fingers spreading as he slid his hands slowly from the waist of her blue sweater down over her hips where the hem of the sweater ended and then beyond. *What do you think?* She badly wanted to ask for details but couldn't seem to make her lips work.

"Here we are," the clerk's voice preceded his return through the swinging door and Wyatt smoothly stepped away from Sarah-Jane, though she could still feel the impression of his fingertips when he'd pressed them warmly against her thighs. He calmly picked up another Castleton boot and studied it while Sarah-Jane waited in vain for the planets to re-align themselves.

She plopped more than sat down on the hard wooden seat and flipped off her remaining tennis shoe to pull on the boot's mate when the clerk handed it to her.

It slid on just as easily as the first. She tugged the legs of her jeans down over both boots. "It seems a shame to think someone will be hiding that beautiful stitch work under their jeans," she said as she stood.

"Your jeans," Wyatt said.

"Wyatt—"

"You want to argue about this?" The faint smile was on his lips, but the look he gave her was wickedly dangerous.

He'd already given her one expensive gift—the shawl. "I can't possibly return such an extravagant gesture." She kept her voice close to a whisper. A *firm* whisper.

"That's the thing about gifts," he whispered loudly back, obviously finding her attempt at subtlety amusing. "They're supposed to be given without expectation."

"Something I'm sure they taught you at that charm school of yours, but something that doesn't really apply all that often in real life." In her exasperation, her whisper disappeared altogether.

While that grin of his seemed to be permanently fused to his lips. "If it makes you feel better, knit me a sweater or something. Or model a crocheted bikini for me." Then he raised his voice so the clerk could hear. "We'll take 'em." He didn't look away from her face. "And she'll be wearing them out."

"Very good, sir." The male clerk was beaming as he scooped up Sarah-Jane's tennis shoes. "I'll wrap these up as well," he said. "Is there anything else I can help you find? Perhaps a cowgirl hat for the lady?"

She was too bemused to do anything but shake her head,

though Wyatt's eyes had turned speculative again. "A hat would be good," he murmured. "What d'you have?" He raised his voice for the clerk's benefit.

"A fine selection," Sarah-Jane muttered in the instant before they heard the clerk call back those very same words. Wyatt was already heading off to follow the clerk, and she snatched the loose fabric of his plaid shirt, tugging him back. "Wyatt, it's really not necessary to spend all this money on me. I'll look silly dressing up with a cowboy hat on. I'm not one of those women who can carry off this sort of thing." She hated, seriously hated, having to point that out to him.

"*Those* women?"

She gestured at one of the posters on the wall of a curvaceous celebrity flirting out at them, wearing fancy boots and a hat and shockingly short Daisy Dukes.

"And I disagree," he said calmly, barely giving the poster a glance. "I think you'll look very *un*silly. And I'm finding it quite necessary."

"*Why?*"

"Has anybody ever spoiled you in your life, Sarah-Jane? And I don't mean spoiled in the negative sense. But spoiled as in—" He broke off, obviously thinking.

"Pampered," the clerk provided, disgustingly helpful as he returned with several hats stacked one on top of another.

She frowned at Wyatt and tugged on his shirt again until he followed her around the tall kiosk of rolled posters for sale. "I don't need *pity* pampering, either," she muttered.

"Oh, for God's—" His white teeth bit off his words. "Have a little pity on me, would you please, and let me do this?" He didn't wait for an answer. "Stay here." He went back around the kiosk and returned a moment later with an off-white wool felt hat with a narrow leather hatband that he planted on her head. Then he practically dragged her back to the mirror by the boots and turned her to face it. His fingers were hard on her hips. "Look at yourself," he said gruffly. "What do you see?"

All she could see was him.

He made a rough sound in his throat and pressed himself hard against her as he angled his head down until his mouth was as close to her ear as the wide brim of the hat allowed. "Keep looking at me like that, and I might not be responsible for what happens."

She'd gone hot all over. Maybe it had been a long time since her one and only experience with an aroused male, but she certainly knew what one felt like when he was pressed up against her. There was just no mistaking some things.

"Look at yourself, Sarah-Jane," he murmured and despite herself, her gaze moved from the reflection of him to her own face. "And tell me. Do you honestly believe you look *silly?*"

She looked. The surplice cut sweater hugged the full jut of her breasts, outlined her waist and accentuated the swell of her hips. Besides that, her painfully tight nipples were standing out against the royal blue cashmere, and her eyes looked dark and needy.

She looked as aroused as he felt against her.

"I didn't expect this," she said faintly, and wasn't even sure exactly what she referred to. The boots and hat. Or the heat from him that she could feel burning right through her clothes.

He exhaled audibly and carefully stepped away from her. "I know you didn't," he murmured. Then he started toward the front of the store. "Ring it all up," he said loudly so the clerk would hear.

"Wyatt."

He stopped. Turned back toward her. "What?" A muscle was flexing rhythmically in his jaw.

She let out a breath, and before she could talk herself out of it, she settled her palm lightly on his chest, leaned up and pressed her lips quickly to his. Her heart was rabbiting around inside her like a mad thing as she went back down on the heels of her ridiculously expensive, impossibly beautiful boots. "Thank you." For the boots. For the hat. For making her feel beautiful and wanted, even if it didn't last. "But will you answer me one question?"

His lashes narrowed, but that only seemed to make the blue of his eyes even more potent. "If I can."

"What do you have planned that I'd need boots and hat for?"

"Riding, of course."

"Horses?" She was surprised, but in hindsight, realized she shouldn't have been.

He, on the other hand, let out a sudden bark of laughter. He scooped up his hat from where he'd left it on the chair and settled it on his head, the brim pulled low over his eyes. "Yes. Horses." His smile looked unholy. "Unless you have riding something else in mind."

Chapter Eight

Sarah-Jane still felt flushed an hour later.

After Wyatt had paid for their purchases, they'd driven out to the Double Crown ranch, owned by his distant cousins, Lily and William Fortune, where she'd been torn between gawking at the size and scale of the Southwestern buildings. He'd stopped in at the main house, a multiwinged structure that struck Sarah-Jane as surprisingly modest in style which was surrounded by a sandstone wall and a glorious garden bursting with native colors.

Before Wyatt had even had a chance to use the knocker on the massive wooden door, Lily had appeared around the side of the house, hailing them. She'd been wearing faded jeans and a denim shirt plus work gloves and dusty boots, carrying a basket full of wild roses and had looked just as exotically beautiful as she had years earlier when Sarah-Jane had first interviewed with her at the Fortune Foundation.

"Wyatt, darling," she'd greeted, setting down her basket and tugging off her gloves to hold them out to him. "I was beginning to wonder what had become of you both. I was hoping you'd get here before William and I head into Red Rock to meet some friends, or those clouds up there decide there's some water in them after all and rains all over your plans." She'd accepted the kiss he dropped on her cheek before turning her smiling welcome to Sarah-Jane, tugging her close for a wholly unexpected hug, before setting her back to cast her gaze over her. "Don't you look just as pretty as a picture, Sarah-Jane. Either The Stocking Stitch is treating you exceptionally well, or this rascal here is." She'd gazed fondly at Wyatt.

Sarah-Jane had felt surprisingly tongue-tied even though she'd seen the gracious woman more than once since she'd first come to Red Rock and had always found her to be extremely nice. "Both are treating me very well, Mrs. Fortune," she'd managed.

"And well deserved, I'm quite certain," Lily had said, giving her arm a little squeeze. "And please, call me Lily. I've told you that before. I won't keep you youngsters. Wyatt, you'll find everything you need in the stables. But if you need assistance, I'm sure Ruben won't be far off." She'd picked up her basket and her garden shears and headed into the house with a wave. After that, Wyatt had taken Sarah-Jane's hand once again and they'd walked some distance past a beautifully weathered barn until they'd reached the stables.

Which is where Sarah-Jane presently stood, staring up at a brown horse that seemed immense to her. She'd seen movies, television shows, where individuals had mounted a horse. She'd just never done it personally.

She gingerly reached out and patted the horse's gleaming neck and his—her?—head swung around to eye Sarah-Jane with patient brown eyes. "Er, Wyatt?"

He was standing behind her, saddling the horse he would be riding—a dark gold mammoth with a nearly-white mane and tail. For the "vice president and financial whiz of JMF financial," he looked entirely at home in the stable, hefting around saddles on his broad shoulder and easily deciphering the tangle of straps that made up bridles and reins. "Problem?"

She braced herself for embarrassment. "How do I get on?"

"You haven't ridden a horse before? And you call yourself a Texan," he teased gently. "Why didn't you say so earlier?"

Definitely embarrassed. "Believe me, I wouldn't have if I knew how to get my foot up in this stirrup here." The thing was about on a level with her waist. Her jeans were comfortable and had a fair amount of give, but not that much. Even without the jeans, she couldn't envision lifting her foot up that high. She'd taken up running, not gymnastics.

He laughed softly. "Don't worry. I'll give you a boost up onto Annabelle there soon as I finish here."

Which just left Sarah-Jane to worry over what a "boost" might entail.

As it turned out, it meant placing the toe of her brand new boot in the hands he linked together.

"Okay," he coaxed. "When you put your weight on my hands, I'll lift. You hold the reins and the saddle horn in your left hand like I showed you and the back of the saddle with your right. Your weight is on your foot so you're pushing up, not pulling up with your hands. Then you just swing your leg over, nice and easy."

She barely heard anything past putting her weight on his hands. "I'm too heavy."

"Oh, for the love of Pete." He straightened, his hands propped on his hips. "You're not too heavy. Honey, I've got eighty pounds on you, easy. I can give you a boost, or I can just lift you up there. What'll it be?"

If he thought he had eighty pounds on her, she didn't want to disabuse him. He was six feet of hard, muscular man. She was five-seven of stubborn, female curve. She knew, because she carried it around every day with her, and it wasn't budging another pound, despite her efforts. Better for him to bear part of her weight than all. "Boost, please."

He smiled slightly and she had the strangest sensation that he'd been reading her mind as he crouched down and linked his hands once again. "Go ahead and grab the horn."

She reached up and wrapped her fingers around the hard, leather covered saddle horn and gingerly set her boot in his hands.

"Okay, now step down and push yourself up."

Holding her breath, she did exactly what he said, and she suddenly found herself rising almost magically upward. That wasn't so bad. She swung her leg over the horse, managing not to kick poor Annabelle in the process, only to keep right on going, sliding off the opposite side and landing in a heap on the straw-covered ground.

She heard Wyatt curse even as laughter warred inside her with the effort to catch her breath. He was beside her in a flash, leaning over her with a mighty frown and running his hands gently down her arms and legs. "Are you hurt?"

She inhaled. Coughed. Let out a laugh. Annabelle even swung her head around to give her a look. "Other than my pride?" She inhaled again. Coughed. Let out another laugh before rolling over and pushing up onto her knees. "Don't worry. I'm fine."

He let out a loud breath. "You scared the hell out of me!"

She brushed at the straw clinging to her sweater. "What can I say? I'm no ballerina."

"I don't know any ballerinas personally so I couldn't say how well they mount a horse, either." Now that his heart was starting to climb down out of his throat, Wyatt angled his head slightly and studied the view she made in front of him. "You missed some straw," he murmured.

She pushed to her feet and craned her head around, pulling at a piece that had stuck in her long, loose hair. "Where?" She swiped her hands down her thighs one more time. "Did I get it?"

Hell. Why not torture himself a little more? He'd been in a world of hurt since she'd opened her apartment door that morning looking like a fantasy. The episode at the Western wear shop hadn't helped him any.

He put one hand on her shoulder and the other on her hip, turning her slightly. Then he swept his hand down over the perfect shape of her luscious rear, brushing away the straw that was clinging there. Keeping his hand from lingering was about the toughest thing he'd done in quite a while, but he managed. Just. "All clean," he muttered gruffly and she snatched up her hat where it had fallen to the ground before hurrying around the head of the horse. He still saw the way her cheeks had gone red.

He followed her and crouched down again. "Okay, this time, keep *hold* of the horn," he suggested wryly. "Or if you're more comfortable, get a good handful instead of Annabelle's mane right here." He patted the horse's neck.

"Oh sure," she muttered, rolling her eyes. "Pull the poor thing's hair right out." But she was still smiling and she quickly set her boot in his hold. A second later, he'd boosted her easily on top of the horse. This time she stayed seated and she beamed down at him.

She was so damn pretty it made him ache inside.

"Push down your heels," he instructed as he adjusted the length of the stirrups. "You don't want your boot sliding forward or getting stuck in the stirrup." Once he was satisfied, he adjusted the clenched grip she had on the reins. "Relax. All you'll need to do is guide by the reins. Annabelle knows what to do." She was smiling all the while, but still he could tell that she was listening closely. And then it was just a matter of getting up on his own mount, and then he led the way out of the stables.

As soon as they were out in the open air, he held up Monty for long enough for Sarah-Jane and Annabelle to come up next to them and they fell into a companionable silence that was broken only by the creak of saddle leather and the occasional jingle of a bridle as they left the ranch buildings long behind. Overhead, fat white clouds drifted lazily through the sky, playing hide and seek with the sun.

He couldn't have ordered up more perfect weather for a day spent riding. Neither too hot nor too cool.

"It's so beautiful out here," she said, as if she'd been reading his mind.

He looked at her. Her dark eyes looked as dreamy as her voice had sounded. "It is." He looked away from her, reminding himself that he hadn't brought her out there to seduce her. He and his brothers had spent so much time in each other's pockets lately, he'd needed some space. From them and from the topic they were all most concerned with—their father and JMF. "So what brought you back from Houston early?"

Her dreamy look vanished. "I'd just had enough."

"Of what?"

"Have you ever had the feeling that no matter what you do, how you look, how you act, it'll never be good enough?" She tilted her head to look at him from beneath the brim of her hat, and he saw her roll her eyes. "Don't answer that. Look at you. You're—" she broke off and wriggled once in her saddle. "Of course you haven't," she finished.

He wondered what she hadn't said. But it didn't really matter, because she was wrong. His father's actions seemed to indicate neither he nor his brothers had been good enough for JMF. Which was exactly the sort of thinking that he was trying to get away from.

"Who's got you feeling like you're not good enough? Your

parents?" She'd gone to Houston for her father's birthday; it was a pretty safe guess. And he felt instant antipathy toward them.

"My mother." She crinkled her nose, confirming his guess, and looked ahead once again. "It doesn't matter. It's too lovely out here to think about it."

"I'm not sure what's worse. A critical parent or one who doesn't say anything at all when they should." He wished he'd just kept his mouth shut when she cast him another look.

"That sounds like you're speaking from experience," she said slowly. "Your parents are in Atlanta, aren't they? Don't you get along with them?"

He knew it was his own fault, opening the door to topics he didn't want to think about. He deliberately focused on the horizon. "I thought we'd head out toward those hills to the west." There weren't a lot of trees surrounding the Double Crown's ranch house, but Lily had told him the landscape was more forgiving up in the gentle hills that was cut through with a small stream. "You up for a little canter?"

Her gaze was so steady it felt uncomfortably like she was seeing right into him. "You go ahead," she finally invited. "I'll plod along and remain safely in my saddle, thanks."

He shook his head, tsking. "Where's your sense of adventure?"

"Still rolling around with my dignity in the straw back at the stable," she said dryly.

"We'll start off slow," he promised.

She made a face. "Great," she drawled, but her eyes were dancing. Her self-worth was haunting in its scarcity—something he was determined to do something about—but she needed no help at all when it came to having a sense of humor.

He clucked Monty into an easy trot and Annabelle agreeably followed suit. Sarah-Jane, on the other hand, scrunched up her face, wincing and laughing all at the same time as she bounced away. "Stop," she begged, splaying her hand across her chest. "I left my running bra at home!"

He did not need to be thinking about her bras, running or otherwise, because all he could think about was getting her out of it. But now he was and there was no help for it. He clucked again and Monty moved from a trot into a canter. Again, Annabelle followed right along.

"Wyatt! You're going faster!"

He shot Sarah-Jane a grin. "Sit your butt down in the saddle," he called. "Cantering is smoother than trotting. Keep the bottom of your spine soft and just rock with the horse. Just like sex," he added, wishing to hell he could rid himself of the devil that made him say it. "All you've got to do is match up your rhythm."

Predictably, her cheeks went red and he heard her make a sort of choking sound, but damned if she didn't settle that God-given rear end down in the saddle. And then he decided he'd better pay more attention to the ground they were swiftly covering than her mesmerizing movements or end up losing his own seat in the saddle.

The horses loped along at a smooth, easy pace until they reached the well-treed hills that Wyatt was aiming for. They stopped when he found the trio of logs positioned on the sun dappled grass next to the thin creek that Lily had described, and he helped Sarah-Jane dismount before he led the horses over to the water. They wouldn't go anywhere, he knew, and he unfastened the saddlebag he'd packed with a lunch from the hotel and handed it to Sarah-Jane. "It's nothing fancy, but it's food."

Sarah-Jane's heart was still bouncing around inside her chest from their ride. She sat down on one of the rough logs that had been positioned in the past by some kind hand and tried not to wince as her tired legs protested. She pulled off her hat and set it on the log beside her, then lifted a leather flap to look inside the bag.

Laughter bubbled out of her. "Not fancy?" She pulled out a cool wine bottle that was wrapped in a clever, padded holder that also had spots for two stemless glasses. "I'd hate to see what you *do* call fancy." How had she not noticed him packing this stuff in the saddlebags?

But then she stopped wondering as she watched him unsaddle the horses. Watching him do *anything* was reason enough to be oblivious to minor details.

He spread the saddle blankets out on one of the other fallen logs and propped the saddles against them before turning toward her. She pulled out the bottle and handed it to him. "I'm surprised you trust me to drink wine again after the last time."

He smiled slightly. "I'll take my chances. But if anyone gets to pretend to be someone else, this time it's me." He slid her a look and stuck his hand into the saddlebag, coming up with a wine opener. "And that was a joke, so don't start cringing or anything."

She was cringing, but hopefully not anywhere he could see. "I know you're joking," she managed. "I'm sure there's no reason you'd want to be someone else."

He grunted. "You'd be surprised." He sat beside her and deftly opened the wine bottle before tucking the opener and the cork back inside the bag. "There's food in there, too," he prompted when she just sat there, looking at him.

She didn't delve into the bag again, but held it against her chest, wishing to heaven that she could read his mind the way he seemed to so easily read hers. "Are you happy, Wyatt?"

His eyes narrowed. Then he slid one of the glasses out of the padded holder and filled it with pale gold liquid, which he held out to her. "Right now I am."

She slowly took the glass. "You sound surprised."

"Not really." He filled the other glass. "That's what being around you does."

Her stomach swooped. She made him happy?

He gently tapped his glass against hers and his lips twitched. "Cheers, Gertrude."

Just that easily, she laughed.

So did he.

And she knew that no matter what happened for the rest of her life, she'd never forget that moment.

"Why don't we see how well the rest of the lunch fared?" His voice sounded gruff after his laughter died.

Wholly bemused, she looked away from his face. "Can you hold this?" She held out her glass and reached into the bag with her other hand. She felt the brush of his fingers against hers as he took the glass and she started, the simple, undoubtedly unintentional impact quaking through her all the way down to her toes. She closed her eyes and drew in a careful breath, glad that her tangled hair was falling over her cheeks, hiding her face from him.

He muttered an oath and suddenly set both glasses on the ground before pushing off the log and striding toward the creekside where the horses were grazing.

Alarmed, she quickly set aside the saddlebag and stepped over the spilled wine glasses to follow. She couldn't believe her bravery when she set her fingertips on his back, squarely between his rigid shoulder blades. "Wyatt? What's wrong?"

If anything, he went even more rigid at her touch. "Sarah-Jane, if you want to have just a picnic here and ride on back to the ranch, no harm, no foul, then you'd better keep your hands to yourself and give me a minute."

She sucked in a breath, her fingers curling into her palm and away from him.

He angled his head and she caught a glimpse of searing blue beneath the brim of his hat before he looked away from her, back toward the creek. "That's what I thought," he muttered. "Are you a virgin, Sarah-Jane?"

Mortified, she folded her arms tightly across her chest. "Why would you even ask that?"

He exhaled noisily. "I'll take that as a yes."

She had a fleeting thought of Felicity, who really was a virgin. "Well you'd be wrong," she retorted, even though her face was flaming hot. "Are *you?*"

He gave a bark of laughter that did not sound in the least bit humorous. "Not since I was still in high school and wet behind the ears."

She lifted her chin. "I guess that'd make two of us, then."

He gave her another look. A disbelieving one.

She automatically glanced up when a drop of water hit her cheek. The clouds had collected together and it had begun lightly sprinkling. "His name was Bobby and he was the captain of my high school football team." The rest of the ignoble details were hers to keep, and frankly seemed to be losing their importance by the minute.

He thumbed his hat back an inch. "Was he, now." His voice had gone smooth. "And who else?"

She pressed her lips together. "A lady doesn't sleep and tell."

"A lady just did," he pointed out calmly, though the ferocity in his expression remained. "Her name was Jennifer and she was head cheerleader."

"Naturally," she muttered sourly. She couldn't have competed with a cheerleader back then any more than she could compete with a beauty pageant winner now. "Followed no doubt by a bevy of Jennifer and Georgianna types."

"None of whom interest me at this particular moment." His gaze was burning over her face again. "Sarah-Jane, do you even have a clue how much I want you?"

That swooping inside her started up all over again. "Maybe.

Sometimes I think maybe you might sort of—" Her throat closed off like a vice.

"Maybe," he repeated softly. *"Might."* He pulled his hat off his head and slapped it hard against his thigh. Then he raked his fingers through his hair and shoved the hat back in place. "Honey, however many men there've been for you— one or a dozen—they obviously didn't teach you squat." He turned and slid his arm around her waist, hauling her up flush against him. "Does this strike you as *sort of?*" His palms ran over her hips and closed over her derriere.

Swooping and turning liquid. She stared up at him, unable to make her tongue work to save her soul.

He closed his eyes for a moment, and then looked at her again. "What am I going to do with you?"

Dumbfounded tongue or not, her hands still worked even though they were wedged between them. She curled her fingers against his ridged abdomen, then managed to slowly inch up the soft white cotton knit of his T-shirt.

His gaze narrowed and he went still. Watching. Waiting.

Hardly daring to breathe, she worked her hands upward, angling toward his shoulders and taking both the T-shirt and the plaid shirt along the way. Only when he eased his hold on her was she able to push her hands right beneath until she splayed them across the hard planes of his chest. The softly crisp hair there tantalized her palms, inciting her to explore just how far it spread.

He suddenly shifted and caught both her wrists in one hand when she started following it downward and pulled away. "Wait."

Disappointment, humiliation, despair. In a heartbeat, they were all clogging together in her chest. She yanked her wrists free and the soles of her new boots slid a little as she hurriedly turned, wanting to race away. Anywhere, but just…away.

She heard him curse softly. "Sarah-Jane, where the hell do

you think you're going?" He caught her arm and swung her back around to face him. "What's going on?"

She couldn't look at him. She felt like she was dying inside. Of course she'd fallen for him. How could she not? But it was foolish to forget she was still who she was. Plain Sarah-Jane. "Just don't lie to me, Wyatt. Please." She could take anything but that.

His fingers closed over her chin, forcing it upward. "Look at me," he said quietly.

She opened her eyes and found her gaze trapped in his.

"What lie am I supposed to be guilty of here?"

She was not going to cry. "You said you wanted me, but—"

His gaze sharpened even more. "But...what?"

"You stopped me," she whispered miserably.

Astonishment drew his mouth slack. Then he ran his hand down his face, seeming to wipe it away. "Sarah-Jane," he said slowly. "One of these days, you've got to stop jumping to conclusions." He shook his head once. "You're no good at it, honey."

"But you—"

"But I nothing," he cut her off. "I didn't *want* to stop anything, Sarah-Jane, but I didn't bring you out here because I expected something like this to happen. Not—" he added, obviously forestalling "—that the thought hasn't crossed my mind. Hell, it's been crossing my mind since I saw you that first night at Red. But all this just brings home the fact that—no matter what sort of experience you say you have—you don't go around indulging in casual sex."

She swallowed hard. "Do you?"

He grimaced. "There've been a few occasions," he admitted with what she suspected was considerable understatement.

"But...but not now?"

He grabbed her shoulders and squeezed hard enough to get her attention. "Because I don't feel casual about you!" His jaw flexed. "And *you* should never feel casual about this sort of thing," he added stiffly.

For an insane moment, she had to stifle the urge to giggle. Or maybe it was a tinge of hysteria. He didn't feel casually about her? What was that supposed to mean?

She chewed on the inside of her lip, feeling utterly out of her depth. "You invited me to your hotel room that night. After you took me to San Antonio." No, he'd invited *Savannah.* "You…felt casual then?"

He looked pained. "Do you want me to lie now?"

Dear heaven. Did she? She slowly shook her head. The fat white clouds overhead were turning even darker and she saw another raindrop fall, this time hitting his shoulder.

He didn't seem to notice. His thumbs roved restlessly over the points of her shoulders. "Yes," he finally said. "I would have slept with you. Not that night, because you were three sheets to the wind and I still have a few standards. But you would've been sober when you woke, and I'd have been there, all right, ready and waiting."

"For Savannah."

His lips thinned. "For *you.* It takes more than a name to get me going, Sarah-Jane. I'd spent hours at Max and Emily's wedding reception watching you. I wanted to put my mouth on every inch of you and forget every damn miserable thing in my life except the feel of your legs wrapped around me."

Her breath stole out of her. "And now?" The words were barely audible, but he still heard.

"Now I still want to put my mouth on every inch of you and forget everything except the feel of your legs wrapped around me," he repeated evenly. "But I won't as long as it feels like I'm taking advantage of you."

A spurt of pride belatedly reared its head. "I was the one trying to take off your shirt," she pointed out huskily. A raindrop hit her hand. She ignored it.

"Yeah. And bringing me closer to the end of my rope." He moved his hands to her head, sliding down her hair until he slowly wrapped his fingers in the tangled strands. "I don't think you have a full understanding of how little control I have where you're concerned."

"I don't want you controlled." The longing thought found voice without her even intending it. But it was out there. She couldn't take it back. And he'd closed his eyes and made a low, groaning sound that sent shivers dancing down her spine. And it made her brave. "I want to feel your mouth on every inch of me," she whispered. "And wrap my legs—"

He let out a harsh breath and covered her mouth with his.

Her legs went weak. Actually, truly so weak she didn't think they'd be wrapping around anything. But it didn't seem to matter, because his hands had gone from her hair to her waist to her derriere again, and he pulled her on to the toes of her new boots, nudging one thigh between hers. Color spun inside every sense she possessed, as vivid and seductive as the reflection of the Christmas lights on the water that night at the River Walk. When he tore his mouth from hers, hauling in a harsh breath, she leaned up, pressing her mouth against the warm column of his throat. Tasted the slightly salty taste of him.

She felt as much as heard the low rumble that rose up from his chest, and then he was kissing her again. And his hands seemed to be everywhere. On her spine. In her hair. Sliding down her hips, delving beneath her sweater, pulling it up, up, up until he had to pull her hands free from where they were buried in his thick hair so that he could pull it over her head.

And when that soft cashmere knit was gone, no longer protecting her, Sarah-Jane froze.

"Look at you," Wyatt breathed, almost reverently, as he settled his palms on her shoulders before sliding them slowly down her arms. "How can you not see yourself the way I do?"

His thumbs glided over the white, weblike lace that covered her breasts, not doing a single thing to hide her achingly tight nipples from the pads of his thumbs.

It was exquisite and she couldn't help the breathy moan that escaped. He inhaled on a hiss and slowly, deliberately slid his index finger along the top of the scanty cups, slipped beneath, and inched the lace below her nipples that sprang free, embarrassingly eager. "You are so beautiful," he whispered, brushing his thumbs over and around and over again, making waves of pleasure pulse right through her. And when he lowered his head and drew one of those tight points between his lips and tasted her there, she shuddered, her fingers desperately clutching at him.

"I like that, too," he murmured, and suddenly, they were moving, until he sat down on one of the big, fallen logs and he pulled her down on to his lap facing him. She exhaled shakily, only to suck air back in when his mouth returned to her breast and she felt his hand sliding up her bare spine. Then the confining lace was gone and her breasts filled his hand, his tongue teasing one nipple and his fingers the other, while his other hand clamped on her hips, urging on that rocking against him she couldn't seem to stop. Pleasure was screaming through her and she couldn't do anything to hold it back, but wind her arms around him and cry his name as she convulsed.

She was still shuddering when she felt him shift, and then not even his T-shirt separated his chest from hers as he held her close. Her heart was hammering. Or maybe it was his, too. She couldn't tell. Didn't care.

He slid his hand up to the back of her head, tucking it against his neck while she tried to regain her equilibrium. But there was no hope for that. Not when she could feel every hard line of his rigid abdomen against hers; feel that insistent bulge pressing so demandingly against the quaking heart of her despite their jeans.

She ran her shaking hand down his belly, felt him flinch when her fingertips reached his fly. He grabbed her hand. "I didn't bring a condom." His voice was rough.

Dismay sank through her. "You...didn't?"

He grimaced. "I told you I didn't bring you out here for this. That's why I was trying to slow things down. But you," he pressed a hard, fast kiss on her lips that made her feel dizzy. "Just keep tempting and tempting."

She thought there surely must be something wrong for feeling so giddy that she *could* tempt him. "I thought guys always carried a, um, one of those things in their wallet."

He gave a snort of laughter that only succeeded in rocking their hips together again. He closed his eyes for a moment, inhaling through his clenched teeth. But Sarah-Jane could only assume that he didn't want her to move away, considering the hard grip of his hands on her hips, which kept her right where she was. "Guys who are on the prowl, maybe. And I'm assuming from your reaction that you're not on the pill."

"No," she managed faintly. "No, um, no reason."

"Right." His palm slid over her rear end, his fingers sliding inside the low cut waist of her jeans.

She caught her breath. "Shouldn't you stop doing things like that?"

"There'll be time to stop when I'm dead." He kissed away a raindrop that fell on her bare shoulder.

Her heart skittered around. "But—"

"I want to touch you." He lifted his head and his blue gaze set off sparks every place it landed. "Do you want that, too?"

The breeze was cold on her naked back and shoulders and the smattering of raindrops even colder, but the rest of her—everywhere she felt him against her—she was hot and melting. Her breasts were crushed between them, abraded deliciously by that swirl of soft-crisp brown hair, and for once in her life, they seemed exactly right. Everything was exactly right. *He* was exactly right. "I want that." She was breathless. "I want more than that."

The corner of his lips tilted slightly. "So do I. But that's gonna have to wait until next time."

Next time. Her mouth ran dry.

He leaned closer until his mouth hovered against hers, not…quite…touching. "Unfasten your jeans, Sarah-Jane," he whispered. "For me."

She mindlessly reached between them again, feeling his tight abdomen against her knuckles as she fumbled with the top button of her jeans. She had to arch a little to work the short zipper down, and he made a muffled sound, his hands tightening again on her hips as she did so. Emboldened, thrilled, she rocked against him again. Deliberately.

He lifted an eyebrow, looking devilish as he slid an arm behind her arched back. "Think you're getting brave?"

She held her tongue between her teeth for a moment and rocked again. "It's sort of like cantering," she said huskily.

He exhaled a slow oath. "I'd blame this new you on wine, but we haven't had any."

"Blame it on you," she whispered. "I don't feel like this from wine, but from *you*." She pressed her mouth against his, teasing at the seam of his lips with the tip of her tongue. "Touch me, Wyatt." Her voice sounded throaty. Wholly unlike her. "Touch me anywhere you want, but please, oh please, kiss me first."

She felt his fingers tangle in her hair, then his hand was on her head, turning her just so while his mouth opened over hers and his other hand wickedly dove between them, slipping beneath her jeans and the scanty excuse of her panties, and his fingers found her.

She jerked and her fingers dug into his muscled shoulders.

The sensations were so exquisitely intense that she could hardly bear it.

"Don't chicken out on me now, Sarah-Jane," he whispered. His breath was hot against her cheek. Her ear. Shivers ripped through her when she felt his teeth gently graze her earlobe. "Just like cantering."

She caught her breath. He was outrageous. Beautiful. And as his fingers slowly swirled, pressed, teased, then delved until her head fell back and she cried out yet again, she knew that right now…he was hers.

Chapter Nine

They never made it to the wine. Or to the sandwiches that Wyatt had brought along from the hotel. By the time Sarah-Jane's sensibilities were beginning to return, the few droplets of rain began to threaten with more earnest. While Wyatt quickly saddled the horses, she shakily pulled on her discarded bra and sweater. When Wyatt crouched next to Annabelle, his hands linked together for Sarah-Jane, she didn't hesitate this time, and let him boost her smoothly up into the saddle.

Then he swung himself up onto Monty's back in a motion that made her more than a little breathless to watch, and they set off back toward the Double Crown at a much brisker pace than they'd left it.

As soon as the outbuildings came into view, the clouds started to let loose and Sarah-Jane laughed breathlessly. Wyatt shot her a grin as he leaned forward in his saddle. "Hold on," he warned her, and she hurriedly tightened her grip around the saddle horn just as Annabelle and Monty surged forward, their gait lengthening. Speeding.

Sarah-Jane clamped one hand on top of her head to keep her hat from blowing off and held on tightly. She quickly realized that as long as she kept her butt hugged deep down in the saddle, it didn't seem to matter how fast Annabelle galloped.

They made it back to the stables without managing to get drenched, and when Wyatt dismounted and came over to help her down, she felt like her face might split from the smile she couldn't seem to tame. The second her boots were on the ground, she threw her arms around his shoulders. "This was the most perfect day I've ever had."

"Really?" He gave her a slow smile. "And here I was hoping you'd think there'd be *some* room for improvement."

She felt her entire body flush. "Well, maybe there could be," she managed sedately.

He laughed softly. Brushed a kiss over her nose and set her away from him. He unloaded the saddlebag, handed her the contents to hold, and started to unsaddle the horses.

Sarah-Jane could have stood there for hours, happily watching him, but a teenaged boy she didn't know came over to relieve Wyatt of the task. "It's my job, Mr. Fortune," he insisted.

Wyatt would have argued, but he could see the way the kid's gaze kept sliding toward Sarah-Jane. Typically, she was oblivious to the gawking attention she was garnering.

He didn't know where the possessiveness came from, but he damn sure knew he didn't want her being the center of some sixteen-year-old's wet dream. He shrugged out of his shirt and tossed it around her shoulders, as if it were any drier than her sweater, even though it really wasn't. Ignoring the surprised look she gave him, he kept his arm around her and steered her out of the stables and back toward his truck, keeping as much to shaded areas as possible.

"Shouldn't we stop to say thank you to Mrs. Fortune?"

"She and William had plans this afternoon, remember?"

"Oh. Right." She smiled up at him when he opened the truck door for her, and something went tight inside his chest. "They're such a lovely couple," she mused as she stretched up to climb inside.

He watched the voluptuous curve of her backside and shoved his free hand into his pocket to keep from reaching out for her. "Yeah, they're great," he agreed absently.

She settled in the high seat, giving him a curious look. "Something wrong?"

"Nope." Except he was apparently no different than the kid in the stables when it came to gawking at her. He closed the door and went around to get behind the wheel, swiping the rain off his face before starting the engine. Almost as if it had been waiting for that moment, the cell phone he'd left in the truck on the console gave a little chime. He glanced at it. Saw the message was from his mother and dropped the phone back on the console.

"Nothing important?"

"My mother." He didn't know why he told her. The words just came out of his mouth. The rain was coming down steadily and he switched on the wipers as he drove away from the ranch. "I still need to feed you."

She gave him a sidelong look. "Is that all you need?"

He choked back a laugh, thoughts about his mother and Atlanta sliding away like magic. "Honey, if I were to get all I needed, neither one of us would be able to walk for a week." Her cheeks went pink and he grabbed her hand to kiss her knuckles. "How about Red?"

"Sure. If that's what you prefer. Or I could fix you something at my place." She didn't quite look at him. "Felicity won't be there. I'm sure she won't come home from the shop until tonight."

"Making candy?"

She nodded. "Getting ready for Valentine's Day."

He wasn't really interested in what her roommate was doing, much less Valentine's Day. "Fix me what, Gertrude?"

Her lips curved. "I guess that depends on what you're hungry for." Her tone was demure. The sparkle in her eyes was…not.

It was all he could do not to pull over right then and there on the side of the road. He studied her for a moment. "Are you sure?"

"Yes." She slid him a look. "Aren't you? I mean, you're the one who was left, um—"

"—hanging?" he provided wryly.

She pressed her lips together and the pink in her cheeks went even brighter.

He grinned and ran his thumb over her knuckles. "Your place it is. I just need to make a quick stop first. Don't I?" He watched her. Her claims of experience aside, he was still painfully aware that she was a babe in the woods compared to him. Even taking into account what had already occurred between them. If he saw one hint of uncertainty, he intended to back off. It might be his undoing, but it would be the right thing to do.

The look she gave him was shy. And so eager that he went hard all over again. "Yes, please," she said.

He couldn't help but smile. "Ah, Sarah-Jane," he murmured. She was the most genuine person he'd ever known. "Don't ever change."

She blinked. Looked surprised. "I—"

Whatever she would have said went unspoken when his phone rang again. Insistently. He wanted to roll down his window and pitch it out on to the road. But Sarah-Jane had picked it up and was peering at the phone's screen. "It says 'Mom.'" She held it up so he could easily see the display. "If she's anywhere near as persistent as my mother, it's probably easier just to take it."

His mother could be as subtle as a breath of air when she wanted. But she'd also raised four stubborn sons and a daughter who was even more headstrong. The word *persistent* didn't even come close. He reluctantly took the phone and answered the call.

"Wyatt, what's this I hear about you wanting to buy property out there?"

Wyatt grimaced. "I guess you've spoken with Victoria." His sister had found him the perfect property, which they'd looked at the previous day. The only hitch was that it wasn't exactly for sale. Not yet, anyway. But Wyatt figured he could talk the owner—a widowed woman who lived in Arizona—around to it. Putting enough money on the table often had that effect.

"Actually, Jace was telling me about it." His mother's voice was tart. "Once Asher got on the line, he confirmed it. Wyatt, darling, you have *got* to get over this bug you've got about your father!"

"Bug?" He bit off the word, too aware that Sarah-Jane was sitting there beside him. "He's betrayed all of us. I think it's a helluva lot more than a *bug*."

"You haven't even talked to him," she said. "James told me you two haven't spoken since before you left for Emily's wedding."

He realized his speed had crept up and lightened his foot on the gas pedal. "He had his chance to explain, more than once, and he didn't. End of story."

"But—"

"I'm driving, Mom. I've got to go."

Her sigh was noisy, even through the phone. "Nothing's going to be resolved like this, Wyatt."

"Tell that to him," he said flatly. "Goodbye, Mom." He

ended the call and wished he could just as easily end the regret swamping him. His mother hadn't done anything to deserve the situation, either.

He shoved the phone back down on the console and saw the concern in Sarah-Jane's face. "Don't even ask."

She winced a little. "Right. None of my business."

Dammit. He raked his fingers through his hair. "That's not what I meant." This is what thinking about his father and Atlanta did. Turned him into a knot of anger that seemed only to loosen whenever he was with Sarah-Jane. Only he was with her right now, still turned on by everything about her from the silky eyelashes curling around her liquid brown eyes to the sweet curves of her ankles hidden underneath the boots he'd bought for her, and that knot was tighter and angrier than ever.

He loosened his death grip on the steering wheel and eased up again on his lead foot. "Just before Christmas, my father—" his jaw clenched over the word "—announced out of the clear blue sky that he intended to sell off JMF."

She absorbed that. "Can he?"

"We're a private company. Family owned. Family controlled." His lips twisted. "And he controls the majority interest. Yeah. He can do it. He *is* doing it."

"Why?"

"Who the hell knows?" He didn't want to talk about it. Didn't want to think about it. But now that he was, he couldn't seem to make himself stop. "If he'd wanted to retire, all he'd have had to do was say so. Shane's already COO. We all knew it's only a matter of time before he steps completely into our father's shoes. But the old man makes his unilateral announcement and seemed to think we'd just sit around giving him our heartfelt thumbs-up."

"I felt a lot better after I finally told my mother what I thought."

"My father knows exactly what I think," Wyatt said grimly. "Exactly what we all think. It hasn't made a difference."

"Do you know who he's selling to?"

He shook his head.

"When he plans to complete the sale?"

Again, he shook his head and he could feel her studying him. He much preferred her looking at him with passion glazing her eyes. "Won't you miss your job there, Wyatt? You've worked for JMF for how long? Since you were in college?"

He'd worked there even before that. The JMF offices had been as much home to him as their real home. "I miss the work," he allowed. "There's no reason why I have to do it with JMF. Why stay and prolong the end?"

"But he hasn't sold anything yet. If all of you stayed, maybe he'd change his mind."

"Once James Marshall Fortune makes up his mind about something, there is no changing it."

She pressed her lips together for a moment. "Sounds familiar," she finally murmured.

It wasn't the first time he'd heard himself compared to his father. Hearing it from Sarah-Jane, who knew nothing about it except for what he'd just admitted, stung more than he liked. "I know right from wrong," he said flatly. "We're all supposed to be part of JMF. But that obviously doesn't matter to him or else he wouldn't be doing what he's doing."

"*Says* he intends to do. You just said he hasn't actually done it yet."

His hands tightened around the steering wheel again. "Believe me, Sarah-Jane. The man means what he says."

"And so do you. You told me that yourself."

He didn't want to argue with her. Didn't want that knot inside him touching anything to do with her.

"What if you found out he has a good reason?" she asked

after a moment. "How would you feel then? Would you want to go back home to Atlanta?"

"Dammit, Sarah-Jane, I don't want to talk about it." He wanted to chew off his tongue as soon as the words escaped and her face turned pale and pinched. He exhaled roughly. "Atlanta is done and over," he said a little more calmly. "Red Rock is a new start. Completely, totally different from everything there."

"Including me?" She twisted his plaid shirt between her hands. "I know I'm not anything like the women you typically see." He gave her a look and even though she flushed, her chin slanted upward, obviously determined. "Felicity looked you up on the internet," she muttered.

"Felicity."

"Fine. I did, too. There were hundreds of mentions of you. You date tall skinny blondes."

For some reason, he suddenly felt immeasurably better. She was jealous. It was as plain as the pert nose on her face. "There were a few brunettes as I recall."

"Right. Skinny ones who looked like they belonged on magazine covers." Her lips thinned. "So why take up with me? I have no illusions about myself, Wyatt. I'll never be skinny."

"God, I sincerely hope not," he returned. "Nothing but sharp, poking angles." They were still beyond the outskirts of Red Rock and he pulled off the side of the road, shoving the truck into park before angling his body to face her.

Her eyes had gone wide and in the rhythmic swishing of the windshield wipers, he imagined he could hear the hard beating of her heart. Or maybe that was just his. "I thought I'd made myself clear, Sarah-Jane. I want *you*. Just the way you are. I want to bury myself inside you, and feel a woman in my arms instead of a stick I have to worry about breaking in half. I want to fill my hands with your rear end and feel flesh and muscle, not jutting bones. When I kiss your breasts,

I want to feel the weight of them, the softness of them, and know every centimeter is you. Only you."

She was staring at him, her lips parted.

Something inside his chest tightened again. "But even more than that, I want in up here." He tapped her forehead with his finger. "I want in there until you can see the same thing that I see. It doesn't matter if you're in cashmere—" he ran his finger down the V on the front of her damp sweater until his finger briefly delved into the warm valley between her breasts "—or in one of those god-awful baggy shirts you wear at the knitting shop." He took his hand away from her before he forgot where they were altogether. "I could lock you in a room with me and make love to you five times a day or just walk you through town where every guy we pass is ogling you. But none of it would matter if you don't start accepting the simple truth. That you are a beautiful…desirable…woman."

"Five times a day?"

He gave a strangled laugh. "*That's* all you got out of that?"

"No." Her gaze shied away from his. "Wyatt, nobody's ever looked at me the way you do."

"I seriously doubt that." He eyed her. "You just haven't been noticing. One of my own brothers described you as stacked." He briefly considered that. "I may have to throw him off a cliff."

She rolled her eyes, but laughed softly. He liked hearing her laugh. Liked watching her laugh. The way her nose wrinkled just so and her eyes sparkled. The laugh could come out of absolutely nowhere and it was always the same. A little wrinkle that made him want to kiss it, and that incredible sparkle that made it so easy to forget the rest of the world around them.

"He doesn't know what I know, though." He leaned across the console and caught her gently pointed chin between his thumb and forefinger. "That as distracting as the exterior is, the interior is even more fascinating."

Her pupils dilated. "I want to believe you," she finally whispered. "It's just...I've never—" She broke off. Swallowed and tried again. "Wyatt, you're an exceptionally nice man."

He made a face. "Do I sense a kiss-off coming? Nice is a death knell, isn't it?"

She ignored that. "You make it so easy to forget that you're completely out of my league."

"Bull," he countered bluntly.

She blinked a little, looking bemused. But then she scrubbed her hands over her face before twisting them together in her lap. She didn't look at him. "If I'm not careful, I'm going to fall head over heels—" the hitch in her voice was almost too quick to catch "—for you, and then where will I be when this whole situation with your father and JMF is resolved?"

"God save me from the convolutions of a woman's mind," he muttered. "There's nothing to be resolved."

"Of course there is!" Now she looked at him, full on. "Until you understand why he says he's going to sell—"

"He *will* sell—"

"—how can you ever make your peace with a life here in Red Rock?"

"Damn it all, Sarah-Jane, I've made my peace!" His shout filled the cab of the truck.

She watched him, wide-eyed and unmoving except for the quick swallow that worked down her lovely throat.

He should have never answered that damn phone.

He wouldn't have blurted out anything about his father. They'd likely already be back at her apartment, finally making love—completely—the way he wanted. He would have nothing consuming his thoughts except for her.

His breath felt harsh in his chest as he checked the mirrors, put the truck into gear and pulled back onto the rain-slick road.

Sarah-Jane didn't speak until they arrived at the apartment. Wyatt hadn't made any stops along the way. She didn't need any more confirmation that he'd changed his mind about finishing what they'd started out by the creek than that. If she were to believe him, he wanted her. *Her.* He really didn't think she was plain Sarah-Jane.

But she'd obviously stuck her nose somewhere it didn't belong. Namely, his life.

And that obviously overruled something as simple as sex. Casual or otherwise.

When he pulled into an empty parking spot, she hurriedly reached for the door handle. "You don't have to walk me up," she said quickly. "You'll get rained on." She felt his gaze, but couldn't bear to look at him. If she did, she was going to start crying.

It was a fine time to realize that she didn't want him only to *want* her.

She wanted the whole thing.

Body, heart and soul.

Because she was in love with him.

The silence between them pulsed. Outside, the rain poured, streaming down over the windows.

"I'll call you later," he finally said quietly.

A vise seemed to close around her throat. *He never said what he didn't mean.* She held on to the thought like a lifeline and nodded before shoving open the door and sliding out.

It was only after she'd made it inside the sanctuary of her apartment that she realized she was still clutching his blue-and-white plaid shirt in her fist, and she slowly slid her back down the door until she was sitting on the floor.

Then, holding the shirt to her face, she finally let the tears come.

He'll call. He said he'll call.

He didn't call.

Not later that day. Or the next day.

Or the next.

Sarah-Jane didn't have the luxury of curling up and hiding, though she wished that she could. Instead, she made herself get up each morning the same way she had been for years. She put on her running gear and went running. The same way she had been for months. She went to work every day. She taught beginners how to cast on and cast off stitches and the difference between knit and purl. She even finished designing the River Walk sweater pattern and posted it to the shop's website where people would be able to download it for free.

But she couldn't bring herself to go back to the park for lunch. Instead, she spent her lunch hours holed up in the office at the back of the store, poking disinterestedly at her salad and compiling internet orders.

Life, after all, went on. Even when you knew that the man you were crazy to fall for in the first place didn't return your feelings, life still went on.

Knowing didn't make it easy, though.

She received proof enough of that when, nearly a week later, he was sitting on the front step of her apartment after she'd finished teaching her Thursday night class.

Her heart wanted to jump right out of her chest and she knew there'd never be enough time left in the world to get him out of her skin.

Her hand curled tightly around the umbrella she was holding over her head. It seemed painfully fitting that it had started raining again just that afternoon when the skies had been dry as a bone since the last time she'd seen him.

"Wyatt." Just saying his name made her ache inside. She walked closer. "What are you doing here?" He didn't have an umbrella. He was just sitting there, letting the rain pour down on him.

"I don't know," he finally said.

It didn't matter that he was breaking her heart.

He looked dreadful.

She angled her umbrella over him, too, not that it would make any difference. He was already soaked. "What's wrong?" She unlocked the door and pushed it open before turning back to him. "Come inside." He stood slowly and she had to adjust the umbrella so he wouldn't knock his head into it. Water beaded off his leather coat. She pushed at him until he went inside and she quickly closed the umbrella, leaving it outside under the small overhang on the porch and followed him. "Hold on while I'll get you a towel." She didn't wait to see if he agreed or not, but raced into the kitchen where she discarded her wet shoes and slicker, and came back with a clean dish towel.

He was standing right where she'd left him, his attention focused on the floor. Water slowly dripped down from his head.

Concern turned to outright alarm, and instead of handing him the towel, she simply spread it over his head and rubbed briskly, as if he were a little boy and not a full grown man who'd tied her heart in knots. Then she dashed it over his shoulders trying to get the worst of the water off his jacket before tugging it off. "Come," she pulled him toward the couch. "Sit down." The front of his collarless linen shirt was wet and so were his faded blue jeans, but she couldn't do anything about them. Not unless she wanted to get him out of his clothes altogether, and she wasn't foolish enough to think that was a good idea. Not after the way they'd left things.

He sat. "I need a drink."

"Of course. Something hot? Coffee?" She felt a hysterical jolt. She was in love with him and she didn't even know if he drank coffee.

He pinched the bridge of his nose. "Drink, Sarah-Jane. As in liquor."

She gave him an uneasy look. "I think we have a bottle of whiskey that Felicity received for Christmas."

"That'll do," he muttered.

"Wyatt, you're obviously upset." Deeply upset if she were any judge at all. "Are you sure drinking is the solution?"

He started to stand. "I'll go find a bar, then."

That would be an even worse solution. "No. Sit." She nudged at him until he subsided. "I'll get you the drink." She practically ran back into the kitchen and rummaged through the cupboards until she found the bottle. It was still sealed. Still had a festive red ribbon tied around the neck. She tore off the ribbon and quickly opened the bottle, found a short glass and filled it part way. She had no judgment whatsoever whether it was a lot or a little, but she dropped a few ice cubes in it anyway and carried it back to him. "Here."

He took the glass and tossed back the drink without so much as a wince or grimace. He held on to the glass. "Just bring the bottle, Sarah-Jane."

She'd never seen anyone look as grim. "Wyatt, you don't drink. Why don't you just tell me what's wrong, instead?"

"I never said I didn't drink. I said I didn't bother trying to keep up with my brothers." When she didn't go to get the bottle, he got up, set her out of his path, and went into the kitchen himself.

She trailed after him. "What's happened? You came here." Even after nearly a week of silence from him, he'd come. "Please," she said huskily. "Tell me what I can do to help."

He filled the glass halfway, and set the bottle down with a thump. He looked into the whiskey, then left it on the table and turned to face her. "You can do this." His voice was deep. Rough. The hands he set on her shoulders to pull her to him were tense. And his mouth that covered hers was urgent. "Open your mouth, sweet Sarah-Jane."

Her head reeled as if she'd been the one to throw back a few shots of whiskey. She mindlessly opened her mouth, meeting his marauding tongue with her own and he groaned, pulling her nearly onto her toes as he pulled her closer. Tighter. His fingers threaded through her hair, wrapping in it, gently tugging, urging her chin up even higher, her head back even farther. He dragged his mouth from hers, ran it down her jaw, her throat.

Her fingers curled, only to realize that she'd buried them in his thick, damp hair. "Wyatt." If she'd ever possessed a coherent thought, the memory of it was becoming increasingly dim.

"I want you." His voice sounded thick. "I've always wanted you."

Then where have you been?

The question swirled in her mind, but it seemed to get lost somewhere in the heat of his mouth on hers.

"Where's your roommate?"

Felicity, Sarah-Jane remembered dimly. "Trade show. She won't be in until late."

"Good." He abruptly lifted her around the waist right off the ground, ignoring the protesting gasp she made and slid his hands beneath her khaki-covered thighs, urging them around his hips. "Bedroom." His breath was harsh against her ear. "Where?"

She could hardly speak past her heart since it had shot straight up into her throat. "Upstairs. To the right."

He strode toward the stairs, but even then he didn't put her down. Just tucked her head against his shoulder to keep her from knocking into anything. Before she could adjust to any of it, they were inside her bedroom and he was following her down right there onto the center of her thick fisherman knit bedspread. She could feel the moisture from his shirt pressing through her white blouse, but beyond that, could feel the warmth of him burning through. She worked her fingers between them, fumbling with buttons, pushing, tugging, until she could reach beyond the damp linen to the man beneath.

She felt his muscles jump and was thrilled. But when her fingertips followed the trail of his chest hair downward, where it narrowed, turned silkier, bisecting the ridges on his abdomen, he let out a muffled curse and circled her wrists in one hand, pulling them away, pressing them gently against the mattress above her head. "Not so fast." His voice was deep, rasping over her nerve endings as exquisitely as the fingertips he drew down the inside of her arm, over her shoulder and between her breasts until he reached the first button of her blouse.

Her fingers curled, but she felt herself melting into the bed beneath her, completely immobile as he deftly flicked each button free before spreading the white fabric wide, as if he were unwrapping a gift. Then his hands moved, sliding around her waist. His thumbs pressed together just above her navel, his fingers splayed on either side of the waist, then his palms swept inward, over her belly, up to cup her breasts. His eyes were narrowed, his gaze white-hot as he shaped his fingers around her. Explored. Teased. Touching everywhere except the centers that pulled together so tightly beneath the sheer mesh covering them that they were nearly painful.

"Don't tease me," she begged.

He pressed his mouth to her temple. Her cheek. Her ear. "How am I teasing you?"

She shifted against him restlessly. "You know exactly how," she accused thickly. His fingertips were gliding back and forth along the underwire of her bra. "*Touch* me."

His gaze caught hers. His mouth hovered above hers. His fingers slid yet again along the band of her bra. "Where?"

She groaned. "You know where."

"Show me," he murmured against her lips. The long fingers trapping her wrists above her head disappeared.

She swallowed. Need was cramping through her, making her desperate. She shakily lowered her hands to her breasts. "Here."

He stroked the top curves of her breasts, well above the scalloped edges of the sheer cups. "Here?"

She wanted to gnash her teeth. She caught his teasing fingers in hers and dragged them over her nipples. It was like lighting a fuse straight to her center. She shuddered. Wyatt groaned. Teasing evidently forgotten, he found the center clasp of her bra and set it free. The sheer cups sprang apart, still molding her breasts within them, and he lowered his mouth to the valley between.

She pressed her head back into the mattress, only to jerk forward when his lips moved again and the heat of his tongue slicked over one crest, then the other. She caught his head in her hands, not sure whether she was trying to hold him to her, or push him away. And all she did was twist her fingers through the cool, damp strands of hair, and groan his name, then jerk a little when she felt the distinct edge of his teeth gently rasping against her nipple.

She was so aroused she could hardly bear it. But then he levered off her, giving those tightening quakes inside her a respite even while his gaze pinned her in place as he unzipped her khaki pants and slowly tugged them down her hips, her thighs. Pushed them right past her curling toes.

She sucked in her bottom lip, fighting the urge to grab a handful of bedspread and yank it over her. But he breathed her name, and just that easily, the urge to hide herself passed. And when she realized that the fingers he was slowly sliding beneath the narrow mesh bands holding the triangles of her panties together weren't steady, either, the shakiness inside her eased, too, leaving only that desperate, liquid ache in its wake.

She could hear her own harsh breath in the silent room as he pulled her panties away. And then his hand returned, gliding over her thigh, sliding inward, inching upward.

She gasped when his fingers grazed over her. Felt flushed to the roots of her hair at the slickness he found.

He just closed his eyes as if on a prayer, and murmured her name again. Then he suddenly moved, yanking off his shirt and shucking his jeans and boxers in one fell swoop. She knew she was staring but couldn't look away as he tore open the packet he grabbed from his pocket and sheathed himself. And then she gasped again when he came down on her once more.

"I can't wait." His breath burned against her ear just as surely as the hands he slid under her hips, tilting her to him. "I just can't, Sarah-Jane. Please don't let me hurt you."

"You'll only hurt me if you stop." Her mouth opened wide against his chest, her tongue tasting the saltiness of him, and then he shifted, taking her in one swift stroke.

She cried out at the startling, sheer fullness of it, and he stiffened, started to pull back, but she twined her arms around his shoulders, her legs around his. "Don't," she begged hoarsely. "Don't leave me."

His arm curled around the top of her head, his fingers tangling in her hair. His mouth found hers in a searing kiss.

And then slowly, so slowly that he would have stolen her heart all over again if he didn't already have it, he moved again.

Gently rocking. Coaxing. Filling. Almost retreating. Then returning again. Over and over until her nerve endings were screaming and she could feel him inside every pore, every cell. And when she wasn't sure she could survive the pleasure a moment longer, he caught her legs, lifting them higher around him, angled deeper, and proved to her that she could more than survive it. Then she heard him groan, heard her own name on his lips as he surged even deeper, and she gloried in it, crying out insensibly as she exploded around the home he'd found in the very heart of her, shattering into a million points of exquisite...perfect...light.

Chapter Ten

It was a long time before either one of them had the strength to move. But eventually Wyatt levered off her enough that she wasn't suffocated beneath him, before finally rolling away. He tugged the bedspread over Sarah-Jane and brushed his lips over hers. "I'll be right back," he murmured.

She wanted to smile. Where would she go? She didn't have a solid bone left in her body.

She realized something was poking her in the back and shifted around until she'd found the culprit. Her utterly pretty bra. She tossed it onto the floor.

She'd be forever grateful to Felicity for the night she'd dragged her to Charlene's. If not for her, she'd have been wearing plain cotton panties and a decidedly ugly bra.

Wyatt returned, seeming a whole lot more comfortable with his brazen nudity than she knew she could ever be. Not that that kept her gaze from latching on to him as soon as he appeared and closed the bedroom door behind him.

The corner of his lips crooked upward in a wry curl. "Look at me like that in another half hour," he suggested.

"Half hour? That's all it takes?"

She loved the dusky color that rose up his throat.

She loved the soft laugh that he gave even more.

And she loved *him* most of all. She still wasn't sure how she'd managed to hold back the words when he'd been inside her. They'd been blasting inside her head.

"Maybe an hour," he allowed. He caught the knitted bedspread in his hands and tugged until she let it go, and pulled it away from her. "Your work, I suppose?"

He meant the thick, off-white bedspread of course, though he wasn't looking at it, but at *her*. "Yes."

"Nice." He smiled slowly. And even satiated nearly to the point of numbness, she felt warmth bloom inside her.

He climbed onto the bed, stretching out nearly from one corner to the opposite, and wrapped his arm around her waist, pulling her back against him. He crooked his thigh against the back of hers, neatly scooting her rear end exactly where he seemed to want it. His splayed hand against her belly stretched from the undercurves of her breasts to well below her navel.

Warmth was most assuredly blooming.

She closed her eyes and pressed her cheek against his arm beneath her. She wanted his fingers to go both higher, and lower, and the depth of her wantonness shocked her. "Do you want to tell me what this was all about now?"

His fingers slid almost lazily upward. "Why can't you believe it's about *this?*" His thumb rubbed over her, around and around, breathing renewed life into her sensitized nipple.

She shivered, wondering how it was that he could touch her there, and yet she could feel it deep down inside her. "I wish I could."

He exhaled. She felt the brush of his hair as he angled his

head to kiss the top of her shoulder. "My father didn't sell off JMF," he finally murmured.

She turned her head to look up at him. "Why do I have the feeling that's not a good thing, after all?" It should have been, but Wyatt was not wearing the expression she'd have expected.

He shifted. Bent his elbow and propped his head on his hand. She rolled onto her back, watching him, and the way he looked at her breasts made her flesh go as tight as if he were still touching her. "Wyatt?"

His gaze slid up to meet hers. "He gave away half the company shares."

"Gave!"

"To some woman none of us have ever heard of."

She absorbed that. "How'd you find out?"

His lips twisted. "Read the press release. Probably about the same time the media outlets were."

"Oh, Wyatt." Dismay filled her. No wonder he'd been in such a state. "I'm so sorry."

"He's gotta be having an affair with her. Or she's got one helluva hold over him about something else."

"What do you mean? Like blackmail? That's a horrifying thought."

"Stranger things have been known to happen to a Fortune."

"What does your mother say about it?"

He grimaced. "She didn't know about his plan to sell until we told her. I doubt he kept her in the loop on *this*. I sure in hell don't want to be the one breaking the news that her husband is a cheat, as well."

"If he's being blackmailed, maybe he's not cheating," she suggested weakly.

"Is it some flaw in your DNA that causes you to go hunting for excuses for people?"

"Not an excuse," she countered. "Just…a reasonable explanation. And I hardly consider it a flaw." At the look he gave her, she turned on to her side and pushed up on her elbow, mirroring his position. "Seriously. The whole point of blackmail is to push someone unwilling into a desired action by threatening to expose some sort of secret if they refuse. If that's the case, your dad might not be willingly giving away anything. You've said he's steadfastly refused to explain himself. Right now, the only thing you do know is the end result. The reasons that led to that result are completely unknown."

"You're sounding like Shane again. He keeps looking for a reasonable explanation, too." His expression plainly showed what he thought of that.

"While you prefer to believe the worst of your father, instead."

"Right now, the only thing I care about is that my brothers and my sister and I have to *live* with the end result. Bad enough to sell right out from under us. But to give it away? The man's spent his life acquiring. Building. Not handing it over to complete strangers. He's betrayed all of us in the worst of ways. Why can't you admit that it's a total BS way to treat us?"

"Why can't you admit that there may be mitigating circumstances that you're unaware of?"

His expression tightened. "I don't want to argue with you about this. I came here because—"

She went still. Waiting.

"—because I wanted to finish what we'd started." His voice turned flat and she couldn't shake the sense that it hadn't been his reasoning at all. If he'd wanted to finish what they'd started, he could have come to her at any point during the past week. But he hadn't.

She'd foolishly fallen in love with him, but that didn't mean she could afford to be even more foolish.

He'd come to her because he was upset. Not because

he'd suddenly realized he was in love with her, too. That he couldn't live without her.

Wyatt said what he meant. And did what he said. If she'd realized nothing about him, she'd learned that.

But this time, he hadn't.

Was she just a way for him to put off thinking about everything? His father? JMF?

She wanted him with her, but not only because he considered her an acceptable distraction.

That was the problem with love.

It seemed to always lead to someone wanting *more*.

How ironic it was, that he was one of the people to convince her that she actually deserved to have more.

"Wyatt—"

"Yo, Sarah-Jane. You awake?" Felicity's cheerful voice sounded through the bedroom door as she knocked once before pushing it open.

Wyatt bit back an oath and managed to sweep the bedspread over them both in the nick of time.

"You're never gonna guess—" Sarah-Jane's roommate's words broke off as she stepped into the doorway and saw them. Her eyes went wide as saucers. Safely covered or not, it was plainly obvious what they'd been doing. "Oh. Criminy." She whirled around and fumbled for the door. "Sorry. Just, um, pretend I was never here." She dashed out, yanking the door shut after her.

Sarah-Jane was covering her face with her hands. "Good grief." She sounded mortified.

"I thought you said she was going to be out late."

"It *is* late."

He eyed the plain round clock on the nightstand beside her bed. "It's ten."

"To some people that's late." She was looking anywhere but at him as she scrambled off the bed and snatched a flannel robe off the hook on the back of the bedroom door. It was almost as if they'd been caught in the act by scolding parents, rather than a grown roommate. She wrapped herself in the robe and turned to face him. "What are you going to do about your father?"

The robe would have been hideous on his late grandmother. On Sarah-Jane it was pretty much criminal. "I've already done it. I'm in Red Rock to stay."

"The end result," she murmured. "And once again, skipping over all the parts in between."

"You think I'm a coward. Is that it?"

"No, I don't think you're a coward," she dismissed softly. "I think you're hurt. You're hurt because of what your dad's done, because it feels like he's slamming you down, and the way you're dealing with it is to draw this imaginary line with him on the wrong side of it, and you staunchly in the right. Wyatt, I know what it feels like to be discounted by a parent. Maybe your father is every bit as wrong as you think he is, but what if he's not? I have a hard time believing that someone who raised you to be as…as *decent* as you are…doesn't have a great deal of decency himself."

"That's just it, Sarah-Jane. You see things in terms of decency. You have no experience in getting completely screwed over."

She winced. "Well, I guess the guy who took me to prom, and then took my pathetically eager virginity afterward, all so he could collect on a hundred-dollar bet with his buddies the next morning might count as a little experience," she said coolly. "I should have at least gotten half the money, don't you think?"

He wanted to swear. "What was his name?"

"Bo—" Her lips clamped shut, obviously realizing what she was giving away. But it was too late.

"Bobby. Captain of the football team?" He didn't need her

to confirm it; he could see the truth in her eyes. And he'd bet his last dollar that there'd been few, if any, other men during the years between. Making love with Sarah-Jane wasn't like anything he'd ever experienced. But he still recognized her *in*experience. She was too unguarded to hide anything, especially her emotions.

When she'd cried out that she'd loved him while she'd climaxed, he'd nearly come undone.

He'd been so lost in her that at first, he almost hadn't even realized what she'd said. And he was certain that she hadn't realized what she'd admitted, at all.

"Your captain was an ass and if you've let him affect the way you think about yourself, then you're letting him get a lot more than a hundred bucks and a spot in hell outta the deal."

She made a production out of retying the thick flannel belt around her waist. "A man who can say things like that to me is a man who also ought to be able to give his own father some benefit of the doubt."

Jesus. And his mother thought *he* was stubborn.

Sarah-Jane positively scared the hell out of him.

He snatched up his jeans and yanked them on. If Felicity hadn't come busting in, he wouldn't have thought twice about spending the night with Sarah-Jane. Maybe, with her in his arms, he would've actually managed to sleep through the night again.

And using her for his own benefit like that, knowing the way she felt, was probably earning him a spot next to the bastard football kid.

"You're leaving?"

"You saying you don't care if your roommate hears us making love through the walls?" Sarah-Jane hadn't exactly been quiet. Admittedly, he'd blatantly relished her unbridled responsiveness. But that didn't mean he wanted an audience listening in.

Her cheeks went red.

"That's what I figured." He searched for his shirt. Found it in a crumpled heap along with her panties under the corner of the bed. He dangled the sexy little bit of sheer white from his fingertip. "Yours?"

She snatched them from him, shoving them in her pocket. "You seem to be amused by something."

He wasn't amused in the least.

He still wanted her. He wasn't sure if he'd ever get enough of her. And it wasn't an easy thing to deal with, particularly after those gasping words she'd cried. Nothing about her was turning out to be easy to deal with, especially the painful honesty in her eyes that warned him those words hadn't escaped only because of the heat of the moment.

Yet, he wasn't looking for love. He wanted to protect her.

He wanted to shake her.

And he wanted to lose himself in the pleasure of her.

He wasn't stupid enough to think he could accomplish it all. Not when he was probably the thing she needed the most protection against.

He didn't consider himself a player, but he'd never *not* had casual sex before. He didn't *do* love. He'd only ever seen one woman at a time; when he was with her, he wasn't with anyone else. But even so, he'd known those other women were no more serious about him than he was about them.

In comparison, Sarah-Jane was a seductive minefield.

Yet he couldn't make himself keep away from her.

He wasn't sure that he wanted to waste more time trying. He did care about her. But love? The very idea seemed crazy.

"What are you thinking?" Her voice was soft. Her gaze was probing. Seeing enough that he felt raw from it.

"I'm thinking if I don't get out of here, Felicity's going to overhear a few things no matter what I intend."

Too aware of the emotion in her expression that she either

wasn't equipped to hide or didn't want to, he yanked on his wrinkled shirt and buttoned it, not particularly caring that two of the buttons were missing. Hiding, no doubt, somewhere among that ridiculously soft bedspread of hers. He left the shirt untucked. His jacket was still downstairs. It'd cover up the rest of the worst. He sat down on the foot of her bed to pull on his socks and boots and gently nudged her out of the way of the door so he had room to get through it.

She looked up at him. Her fire-kissed hair was a tangled mess, sticking out on one side where she'd tucked it behind her ear. Her cheeks looked red from his whiskers. And she was about the most beautiful thing he'd ever had looking up at him with such trust.

"Are you going to be all right?"

"I'm a Fortune," he said dismissively. "We're always all right."

Her gaze just remained steady on his face.

· He supposed it might be comforting to have someone seem to see right into you. But he was quickly realizing it was also damned uncomfortable. "I'm a Fortune," he repeated. And this time they both could hear all the weight that came with the name in his tone. "Not being all right isn't allowed."

She stretched up on her toes and pressed her lips to his cheek. Then the other, before tugging his head lower until she could softly kiss his forehead. "The only thing I care about is that you're *Wyatt*," she said softly.

He steeled himself when she hesitated. Decided he'd better just kick Captain Football to the back of the line, because he was suddenly terrified that she'd say those three little words. Now. Not in the grip of an orgasm, but fully intentionally.

And he…he was afraid he didn't have those words to give. He'd never said them to a woman who wasn't his mother or his sister. Never wanted to. And now, with them blocked away inside him, as sure as the sun rose every morning, he'd lose her because of it.

His chest tightened.

Her fingers smoothed over his forehead. "And that you're happy with the choices you're making," she finished even more softly.

His knees actually went weak. Hell was going to be too good of a place for him. "Red Rock is my choice."

"Okay." She lowered back onto her heels. There was a small smile of agreement on her lips and a world of disagreement in her eyes. But she didn't say anything more. Just stood there twisting mercilessly at the ugly flannel tie around her waist.

If he stayed, they'd either argue or make love and right then, he couldn't handle more of either.

So he pulled open the door and she followed him downstairs.

There was no sign of her roommate. Poor kid was probably hiding somewhere, trying to scrub out her eyes.

The whiskey was where he'd left it. He pulled on his jacket and contented himself with a fast kiss on Sarah-Jane's cheek, before letting himself back out into the night.

He practically gulped in a lungful of cold, damp air.

He'd escaped.

He wished to heaven he could figure out from what.

The next day, Sarah-Jane returned to the park. She hadn't heard from Wyatt since he'd left her apartment the night before, but she was certain, absolutely certain that he'd come to see her at the park.

But the only one occupying the bench she'd come to think of as theirs was a wizened old man with a cane and his newspaper. She hovered there long enough waiting for Wyatt to appear to know that the old man wasn't there to feed the birds, either. Every time one hopped close, he waved his cane and muttered crankily until it hopped away.

She scattered her seed in the grass and glared at the man when he started to wave his cane. Then she stood there protectively until all the birds had scarfed up their fill before she carried the peanut butter sandwich and apple she'd packed for Wyatt back to the shop with her. She reminded herself that she ought to know better than to make assumptions.

But she didn't hear from him that afternoon, either. Or that night.

On Saturday, trying to pretend she felt perfectly comfortable doing it, she called his hotel. But the phone only rang and rang and rang until an automated message requested she leave a message. She hung up quickly, afraid she'd sound too anxious.

On Sunday morning, she called his cell phone number that he'd programmed into her phone that one day. It seemed so long ago even though she knew it really wasn't. The line didn't even ring, but went straight to his voice mail. Trying to ignore the hollow feeling that had been growing in the pit of her stomach since he'd kissed her on her cheek— her *cheek!*—after they'd made love, she quickly spoke. "Hi. It's Sarah-Jane. Just, uh—" falling apart, obviously "—just checking in to see how you are. Your sister came into the shop the other day. Victoria." She thumped her fist against her forehead. Of course the man knew who his sister was. He only had the one. "Anyway, just thought I'd give you a buzz." She ended the call, and dropped her head onto the kitchen table with a thunk.

"Come on," Felicity said behind her. "You're not hanging around here moping. Come to the shop with me. At least you'll be busy."

Sarah-Jane lifted her head. "Why not? Anything's better

than sitting around, waiting pathetically for the man I'm in love with to contact me."

"Gee. Thanks." Her tone was dry, but Felicity's eyes were filled with sympathy. "I'm sure he's just been busy," she added. "Or maybe he's gone to talk to his father. I know how much you believe he needs to."

"Maybe." If she said it often enough, would it seem more believable? Wyatt's opinion about his father's actions seemed set in stone.

When her cell phone buzzed later that afternoon, everything inside her leaped for joy. She eagerly put the phone to her ear, only to hear her mother's voice and not Wyatt's at all.

"I might as well tell you that I know all about this Wyatt business," her mother said as soon as she'd gotten the requisite "hello, how was your week" out of the way.

Sarah-Jane went out the back door of the candy shop for some privacy. "What do you mean?"

"The picture's on the internet, Sarah-Jane. He's in Arizona with some tall blonde woman." Yvette's voice actually softened. "I could have warned you, honey. Men like that don't settle for women like us."

Sarah-Jane pinched her eyes shut. She wouldn't believe it. He'd have an explanation. "Did some man like that break your heart, Mom, before you met Dad?"

"Don't be ridiculous, Sarah-Jane."

And she sighed. Because even if some man *had*, she doubted that Yvette would ever want to—or be able to—share it with her daughter. "Wyatt's there on business." She childishly crossed her fingers against the apron tie behind her back. "I'm going to let you go, because Felicity needs my help at her shop, okay?" She didn't wait for a response to that second, blatant lie. "I love you. I'll talk to you next week."

She pushed the phone into her pocket and went back inside. When she told Felicity what her mother had said, her friend's blue gaze widened. "I don't believe it."

Sarah-Jane appreciated the confidence.

But later that night, when she was alone in her bedroom and her cell phone had remained silent all that day, she turned on her laptop.

The photograph was the first one that popped up as soon as she typed Wyatt's name in the search engine.

A news item, from a Phoenix paper, covering the opening of some new museum there.

The latest woman was blonde. Tall. Skinny.

Everything that Sarah-Jane was not.

Wyatt's hand was on her arm. He was wearing sunglasses, but there was a smile on his face.

She knew him well enough to recognize that the smile was a real one.

She slowly closed the laptop.

Climbed out of bed and exchanged the blue-and-white plaid shirt she'd been wearing for one of her old, familiar Stocking Stitch polos.

She thought about throwing the plaid shirt away. Maybe it would make her feel better if she did. But the ache inside her went much too deep to be salved by something so easy. Instead, she placed it carefully in the laundry bag. Once she'd washed it, she'd make sure it was returned to where it belonged.

Like other wishful dreams, she'd already held on to it for too long.

Chapter Eleven

"Sarah-Jane, niña, you have someone here to see you." Maria spoke softly since there were a dozen women crowded around Sarah-Jane in the work area, knitting and gossiping away.

A customer, Sarah-Jane assumed, and handed the knitting needles and stitching she'd been assisting with back to the teenager who'd accompanied her mother and her three aunts all the way from Dallas. "Remember," she reminded the girl, "count your stitches before you go on to the next row." She patted her shoulder as she pushed away from the table. "Otherwise, you're doing really great. I wish I'd have learned how fun knitting could be when I was your age. All your friends are going to want you making them all sorts of things." She winked. "Maybe even a crocheted bikini."

The shy girl looked hopeful as she caught her lip between her teeth and focused on her project. The girl's mother sent Sarah-Jane a grateful smile.

Maria had disappeared seemingly into thin air, and Sarah-

Jane carefully worked her way around the extra chairs they'd set up to accommodate the large group, and headed toward the front of the store. But the smile that she had automatically pinned to her face faded when she saw no knitting customers browsing in the front of the shop.

Only Wyatt, standing there wearing a dark blue suit and red tie, carrying a leather briefcase.

Every nerve she possessed jangled with alarm as well as about a million other things that were simply too painful to think about.

He didn't look like the Wyatt she knew.

The Wyatt with faded jeans and casual shirts; with a battered leather jacket and worn boots. The man she'd thought she'd understood.

She pushed away the thought. "You look like you've just come from a business meeting," she greeted. She didn't know what else to say.

The last time they'd spoken, her body had still been pulsing from his lovemaking.

Seven days ago.

It would have been funny if his repeated absenteeism weren't so painful.

"More or less."

She realized he was referring to her business-meeting comment. His hair was brushed back from his face. As handsome as he looked, she still thought his face looked weary. Or maybe that was wishful thinking, too. That he felt as worn down as she did.

"I was over at the Fortune Foundation," he added. "You haven't been in your park."

She wanted to ask him what he'd been doing at the Fortune Foundation, but didn't. She'd learned her lesson, asking questions of him that were too personal. Taking everything too personally. He'd said he hadn't felt casually about her and from then on, her foolish heart had started knitting fantasies out of thin air. "We've been busier than usual here." It was true enough. The shop was keeping them busy. Particularly since she'd finally managed to let go of Carmen, though she'd first arranged a more suitable job for the girl with the local parks association. There Carmen would be able to put in more hours and earn that extra money to help feed her family that she'd been so desperate for that she'd felt compelled to slip money from the knitting shop's till. "I've been working through my lunch hours," she added.

He didn't look as if he believed her, but he didn't push the matter. "I've got something I want to show you."

"Why?"

"Not *what?*" He sighed a little. "Please, Sarah-Jane. It'll just take an hour or so. Can you get away from here?"

"Of course she can," Maria inserted, appearing out of nowhere. Her smile was beatific; completely oblivious to the look that Sarah-Jane gave her. "She can have the entire afternoon, in fact." She patted Sarah-Jane's arm. "It's not as if you ever take any time off, niña."

Left with no graceful way out, Sarah-Jane retrieved her purse from the office and went outside with Wyatt. But there she stopped. "I'm sorry, Wyatt. But I really don't want to go anywhere with you."

He looked pained. "I deserve that. I know. Just…please."

She needed to turn on her heel and walk away. But if she did that, he'd know how much he'd hurt her. And somehow, it was suddenly important that she not give him that, too. Another thing she'd learned from him. So she stepped over to the truck that he'd parked in front of the shop. He opened the door for her and not even refusing to draw breath could mask the incredible smell of him as she climbed inside. He tossed his briefcase behind her on to the seat in the back and went around to get behind the wheel.

But he didn't immediately start the engine. "How have you been?"

She kept her gaze glued out the front window. "Fine," she lied without a speck of regret. "You?"

"You have dark circles under your eyes."

She could say the same about him. "How nice of you to point that out." She knew she sounded bitchy, but couldn't seem to help it. She exhaled. "What do you want from me, Wyatt?"

"More than I ever expected," he murmured, more to himself than Sarah-Jane, or so it seemed to her. He started the truck and pulled smoothly out into the light traffic. "I told you. I want to show you something."

The answer was no more satisfying than it had been the first time. She stared out the side window and reminded herself that she had no reason to feel one iota of anything pleasurable or hopeful just because he'd come around again. Given his proclivity for disappearing, he'd undoubtedly soon be off again. "How are your brothers?" she asked, just to make conversation.

"Fine. I haven't seen them since I got back to town this morning. I've been in Arizona. I was there for a few days."

She frowned. More like a week. She nearly called him on it, but controlled the impulse. Just as she controlled the impulse to tell him he'd have been better off going to Atlanta and resolving the situation that had driven him to Red Rock in the first place. "What's in Arizona?" Asking was like picking at a raw wound.

"A ninety-year-old woman named Gertrude."

Her head swiveled around. "Excuse me?"

He shrugged and gave a smile that, in her opinion, was distinctly shy of humor. "I know. Who'd expect it? Gertrude Leyva, actually. She's an art historian and she's not quite the most stubborn woman I've ever met, but she's close."

Sarah-Jane clamped her lips together, squelching the questions that rose inside her. She turned and looked out the window again.

"I should have called."

Pain sliced through her with all the finesse of a dull knife. "Why? You don't owe me a single thing."

"Dammit to hell, Sarah-Jane." His voice was tight. "You're not making this any easier."

A dozen dull knives, she thought, aching. She looked at him. "Making what easier?" Ever since she saw that internet photo, her heart had been slowly, steadily shattering. Seeing him now, she could still feel shards tumbling.

"Trying to make things right with you."

"Why?"

A muscle flexed in his jaw. Regardless of the dark smudges beneath his brilliant blue eyes, he looked so incredibly handsome that it was hard to bear. "Because I need to be able to make something in my life right."

She shouldn't have any tears left but she felt them burning behind her eyes anyway. "I'm a big girl, Wyatt. You don't have to worry about me just because we slept together."

"Maybe I want to worry about you."

She couldn't afford to believe that. Nor could she think of an appropriate response so she just stared blindly out the window again. She was vaguely aware that they'd driven right out of Red Rock and she hadn't even noticed.

In fact, they were heading in the direction of the Double Crown. But she couldn't for the life of her think why he'd want to take her back there. She pleated the worn strap of her purse and tried not to think about it.

As it turned out, he drove right on past the turnoff for the Double Crown. She had no idea how far, but guessed they'd gone at least several miles when he pulled off on a rough road that seemed little more than a coyote path to her.

They jostled along for a while and then he turned again, heading up a gentle incline and finally stopping right in the middle of nowhere. He got out of the truck, came around and opened her door. "What do you think?"

Confused, she looked from his tense face to the expanse of land spread out below them. "Think of what?"

He unsnapped her safety belt and curled his hand around hers. "Come."

Nerves jangling, she slid out of the truck and immediately pulled her hand away. She was wearing tennis shoes, jeans and a new, pale pink Stocking Stitch T-shirt that even Felicity had praised, and she felt oddly dwarfed by him.

But then he moved back, giving her space as if he sensed her need for it, and waved his hand at the horizon. "What do you think of the view?"

She thought he looked as weary as she felt. But she knew he wasn't referring to himself, and she turned her gaze away from him. The view in front of her *was* lovely, dipping down on the other side of the hill where they stood, offering a gently rolling spread of wild grass. There were more hills off to the east full of trees. They reminded her too much of the hillside where they'd gone horseback riding and she looked away, instead watching a hawk swoop lazily through the air. "It's a beautiful view," she said without emotion.

"Then our bedroom window should face it."

She heard the words, but couldn't seem to make sense of them. "Excuse me?"

He put his hands on her shoulders, angling her just so, until she had that distant hillside square in her line of sight again. "Those are our trees, Sarah-Jane," he murmured. "I can't lay claim to a deed because they stand on Double Crown land, but they're ours all the same."

"Wyatt," she whispered. "What are you trying to do to me?"

His arm came across the top of her shoulder, finger pointing from the trees on the east to a point just as far to the west. "That's how far the land goes, Sarah-Jane. There's room for us. For my brothers. For us all to make new homes. New lives. All I need to know is whether you like it as much as we do."

She heard him. But the words "our bedroom" were still ringing around inside her head. "You bought it?"

"I'm going to." His hands left her for a moment and he pulled his cell phone out of his pocket. He punched a few buttons. "Mrs. Leyva? Wyatt Fortune." Sarah-Jane watched his lips twitch. "She likes it, so we have a deal. That's right. Cash. Just like we agreed this morning." He named a sum that prompted Sarah-Jane to feel an urgent need to sit down. "My attorney will be in touch with your granddaughter to handle the rest of the details of the sale."

Cash. Good Lord. She did need to sit. She twisted from beneath his hand on her shoulder and went back to the truck to sit shakily on the running board.

Wyatt followed her, though he was still speaking to Mrs. Leyva. "It's been a pleasure, Mrs. Leyva. All right. Gertrude. You do drive a hard bargain, ma'am." He chuckled at something she said. Then he was telling the woman goodbye and sliding the phone back in his pocket, giving Sarah-Jane a wary look. "What's wrong?"

"You're actually going to buy this land."

"I have bought this land," he corrected. "As of now, Gertrude Leyva and I have a deal. After the dickering she subjected me to for the past week, you can believe I'm going to hold her to it. All that's left now is the paperwork which, fortunately, the attorneys can take care of."

"Plus a not insignificant exchange of *cash,*" she reminded. "How rich *are* you?"

"Rich enough," he dismissed. "Why are you so pale? You said you liked the view."

She gaped at him. "Wyatt, you disappeared for a week.

Again!" He'd been absent from her life almost as long as he'd been in it, if the truth be known. Though knowing it didn't seem to lessen the impact he'd had on her. "Then you just appear out of the blue, drive me out to the middle of beautiful nowhere and bandy around phrases like *our bedroom*." She suddenly pushed to her feet and jammed her palms against his chest so hard he actually fell back a step. "You're darn lucky I'm only *pale* and not collapsed in an unconscious lump on the ground." Her voice rose even more. "What on earth are you thinking?"

Wyatt eyed Sarah-Jane's temper-filled face. "I was thinking that as long as you liked the view as much as I did, this is where I want to build our house."

"*Our* house." She tore her fingers through her hair, which had been smoothed back from her pale face in a sleek ponytail, leaving it in complete disarray. "You have got to stop saying things like that!"

"Why?"

She stared at him like he'd sprouted another head on his shoulders. "Because there is no *our*."

He deserved that. He knew it, but he still felt like he'd been kicked in the gut. "I thought you'd want there to be."

Her mouth opened. Closed. She turned away, started to rake her fingers through her hair again, only to get caught on the band trying valiantly to hold it in place. She ripped it off and her hair swung down past her shoulders, smooth and glossy and winking red fire beneath the bright sunlight.

He wanted to reach for her. Even started to, but shoved his hands into the front pockets of his trousers instead.

Finally, she turned to face him. Her face was calmer. She propped her hands on her hips and he tried not to notice the lush swell of her breasts or the high points of her nipples that were staring up at him, taunting him through her thin, snug T-shirt. What had she done with her baggy polos?

"I didn't think I'd ever hear from you again, and then you spring *this* on me. Wanting to live together when we've only ever slept—"

"I don't want you just living with me. I want you to marry me."

Her eyes widened. Her face went white.

Not exactly the reaction he'd hoped for.

"Wyatt," she whispered. "You can't just propose to me because you're running away from what happened in Atlanta."

He stared at her. "That's what you think?"

She raised her hands. "What else *can* I think? Don't bother telling me you're in love with me!"

His mouth opened. Closed. Definitely not going the way he'd hoped. "Would that be so impossible?" He'd spent the past week away from her, facing the fact that he did.

But pain had dropped over her face like a shroud. She didn't answer. "Did your father explain why he gave away those shares in JMF?"

Inside his pockets, his fists curled tighter. "No."

"Have you tried to talk to him again?"

"There's nothing to say."

"Because you still refuse to consider the possibility that he could have a good reason for his actions?" She pinched the bridge of her nose, exhaled, and dropped her hand again. When she looked at him, her eyes were wet. "Wyatt, if you—and your brothers—if all of you want to make new lives in Red Rock, then do it. But I can't be a part of it."

"You said you loved me."

"What?" She looked appalled.

"When we made love. You said you loved me." He refused to believe he'd been so wrong.

Her throat worked. She shook her head sharply. "If I did marry—" she seemed to stumble over the word "—you, assuming that you didn't just *disappear*—"

He winced, but allowed her the shot. Mostly because she hadn't denied loving him. She hadn't confirmed it. But she hadn't denied it, either.

"—*Some*day, sooner or later I—or our children—are bound to make some decision or some mistake you won't like. What then?"

"You want children?" His thoughts ran off on a tangent, imagining brown-eyed little girls as unexpectedly consternating as their mother and little boys as wild as he'd once been.

"Yes." Her voice was a longing sigh. Then she shook herself. "That's not the point! The point is, what happens when we're not able to live up to your ideals of right and wrong? Are you going to cut us out as easily as you've cut out your father?"

"That's entirely different," he dismissed flatly. "It's my *life* he's messing with."

She stared at him sadly. "It would be *our* life you're messing with if you can't learn to recognize that not everything is always as black-and-white as you think. I've already had a taste of what it feels like for you to just go off somewhere, and we're not even truly involved!"

It had felt pretty involving to him. "I wouldn't do what he's done."

"No. You just walk away for a week now and then." She pressed her lips together. Her gaze slid over the landscape around them. "I don't know what to make of you, Wyatt. I never wanted to believe that you'd—" She broke off. Shook her head.

"That I'd what?"

"It doesn't matter. You never made any promises to me. I know that. I just didn't realize how quickly you'd move from one—" her lips twisted "—conquest, to the next."

"Conquest!" He figured he owed her some latitude. But this was a different kettle altogether. "I never treated you like a conquest." Never once thought of her in those terms. He'd never thought of any woman in those terms.

Her eyes suddenly flashed and with her hair streaming behind her, she looked like some magnificent fury sent from the heavens. "Who was the tall, skinny blonde in Arizona, then?"

"What?"

Her teeth bared. Clenched together. "The one whose picture is blasted all over the internet with your arm around her! I guess you only said all that about sharp angles and bones sticking out when you were taking pity on poor, plain Sarah-Jane!"

"The only people I saw in Arizona were Gertrude Leyva and her granddaughter, who also happens to be her lawyer. And getting them to meet with me in the first place wasn't easy. Getting them around to thinking that selling this land to me was a good idea was even harder." He clamped down hard on his own temper. "I don't know what the hell picture you saw, but whatever it was, it damn sure didn't show me out making some goddamned *conquest!*"

Her chest was heaving with the hard breaths she was drawing. "Then why couldn't you just pick up your phone, Wyatt? You know. Just one call is all it would have taken. A simple, hey, I'm in Arizona trying to buy up a little land." Her eyes glittered and her jaw set. "I never expected every minute of your time, Wyatt." Her voice went hoarse. "If you were finished with me, you could have just said so!"

"I just asked you to marry me. Does that sound like I'm finished with you?" He clawed at the tie strangling his throat and ripped it off to shove in his pocket. "You're the one who evidently thinks I'm not fit husband material."

She looked at him. "You just *left,* Wyatt. No word. No anything. How could you do that if I actually mattered to you?"

"Because you scared the hell out of me! I didn't want to face how much you *did* matter!"

Her gaze lowered. She gnawed on her lip. "And I'm supposed to believe that suddenly, out of the clear blue sky, you have."

"When did you figure out you were in love with me?" Only a week ago, he'd been afraid to hear her tell him the words. And now, he was afraid that she wouldn't.

"When you took me out there," she finally said huskily, and nodded toward the distant trees. She blinked and a tear slid down her cheek. "One minute I just wanted you to want me." Her wet gaze slid to his. "And the next I realized I wanted it all."

"I'm offering it all, Sarah-Jane. Everything I am. Everything I have. It's yours. All you have to do is say yes."

She covered her mouth. Looked away. Shook her head. "I'm sorry, Wyatt. I…I can't."

"You're saying no to my proposal." He didn't know why he needed clarification. Her answer had already knocked the life out of him.

"Was it really a proposal?" Her voice was barely audible. "Or an escape plan?"

He looked at her, standing right in the very spot he'd let himself think their future could begin. Only there was no future. Not with her. "I guess there's nothing left to do but take you home, then." He finally roused himself enough to state the obvious.

She didn't answer. Just looked away and swiped her hand quickly over her cheek.

His chest ached. "I never wanted to make you cry, Sarah-Jane."

She blinked hard. Gave him a shimmering brown look. "I know you didn't, Wyatt." She swiped her cheek again and turned away, heading for the truck. Quiet dignity seemed to roll off her in waves as she climbed up on to the high seat.

He, on the other hand, just wanted to beat the hell out of

something. He tore open his collar so roughly the button popped off, reminding him with vicious glee of the buttons he'd left in her bed, and followed her.

In silence, he drove her back to her apartment. She gathered up her purse that looked like it should have retired a decade ago and looked at him. "Take care of yourself," she whispered and pushed open the door to leave.

"Sarah-Jane. If I'd have called you, would you still be saying no?"

Her eyes closed. She pressed the tip of her tongue to her upper lip for a long moment, seeming to be hunting for something. Strength, maybe. Then she nodded. Just once, before slipping out of the truck and hurrying up the walkway to her apartment door.

She could forgive him for being a cowardly fool.

But she couldn't trust that he would never cut her out of his life the way she believed he'd cut out his father.

Chapter Twelve

"Wait a minute." Asher was staring at Wyatt with shock. "You *proposed?*"

Wyatt threw his briefcase down on one of the couches arranged in the common area of their hotel suite. "You proposed once to a woman yourself."

"And look how well that turned out," Asher reminded flatly. "If I've learned anything, it's not to push a woman before she's ready! Lynn wasn't ready for marriage and she certainly wasn't ready for—" He bit off his words, giving Jace—who was sitting at the dining table by the windows coloring in a book—a telling look. "For the rest," he finished.

Wyatt thought there was a world of difference between Sarah-Jane and his former sister-in-law. Sarah-Jane, for one, didn't have a selfish bone in her body. Considering the way Lynn had walked away not only from Asher but her own child, Wyatt tarred her with the blackest selfishness.

"You've only known her a few weeks."

"So?" He still felt like beating something.

Asher lifted his hands peaceably. "So, nothing. Just an observation."

"Doesn't matter anyway. Like I said. She turned me down. Flat."

Asher was silent for about a half a moment. "Guess that must feel a little new for you."

Wyatt tore off his suit coat and dumped it in a heap. Until he'd gone to Arizona, he hadn't worn a suit since Emily's wedding. He couldn't say that he'd missed it. If accepting the job he'd been offered with the Fortune Foundation meant wearing one every day again, he might have to rethink it.

He removed the preliminary papers he'd taken to Arizona out of his briefcase and handed them to Asher. "It's a done deal, soon as everyone signs on their dotted lines." It was a lot more complicated than that, which Asher knew, but there was no need to explain that to him. "The map of the property is in there, too. Divide it up however you all decide."

Asher slowly took the papers. "You still want the two acres on the ridge, don't you?"

If he wasn't looking out on that view with Sarah-Jane beside him, what did it matter? "Divide it up however you want," he said again. He headed across the spacious room toward the bedroom he'd been using.

"Wyatt." Asher's voice stopped him. "Why did you propose to Sarah-Jane?"

"Because I'm happy when I'm with her."

His brother swore softly, realization dawning. "You really *do* love her."

The fact that Wyatt did, whether he'd learned it too late or not, was moot. "She turned me down, remember?"

"Did she say why?"

And then some.

Asher must have been able to read the answer in his face. "So what are you going to do about it?"

"There's nothing to do! She said *no!*" He slammed his hand against the doorjamb and the wood splintered. He swore again only to realize Jace was watching him with alarm.

"Everything's okay, Jace," Asher was telling his son. "Uncle Wyatt's just a little…frustrated."

Wyatt sank down onto the closest couch and dropped his head between his fists. Frustration would have been easy compared to…this.

"Do you need a hug?" Jace asked in a small voice.

Wyatt's throat burned. "Yeah. Sure." Any port in a storm, even when it came in the form of his little nephew. He opened his arms and Jace darted in for a quick hug, over and done with far too quickly for Wyatt's needs.

He watched the boy scurry back to his coloring. "Ash, do you remember the last time you ever hugged Dad?"

His brother considered it. Shook his head. "Can't say I do."

"I do," Wyatt murmured. "He gave me a hug when he promoted me to VP." The memory was as clear as if it had been yesterday. "Why'd he bring us up to run JMF and then just give it away?"

Asher threw himself down on the couch opposite him. "That is the million-dollar question, isn't it?"

"Do you think he's got a good reason?"

Asher studied him. "I've always thought he has a reason. Whether or not it measures up to your standard of 'good' is another matter."

It was pretty much the same thing that Sarah-Jane had said. "How do you make a woman love you, Ash?"

His brother's lips stretched into a humorless smile. "I'm not sure you can. And even if she does love you, unless you figure out how to give her what she needs, it's not always enough."

Sarah-Jane had told him, time and time again, what she'd needed. He'd just been too stupid stubborn to listen, thinking that anything to do with Atlanta was only about him.

He pulled out his phone, peered at it for a moment, thinking, then dialed.

"Who you calling?"

"Tanner Redmond." Their cousin, Jordana, was married to him. "I can't think of a faster way to get to Atlanta than hiring one of his charter jets."

"Go." Maria swiped her hands in the air as if she were trying to sweep Sarah-Jane right out of the office. "You're spending too much time inside, niña. We won't go out of business if you don't print those orders right this minute. Go out and get yourself some sun. Sit in the park."

Sarah-Jane didn't want the park. Didn't want the sun. She wanted to bury her head in the sand and forget that she'd ever fallen for Wyatt. That he'd offered her everything and she'd tossed it in his face. She wasn't plain Sarah-Jane. She was just plain stupid Sarah-Jane.

"Wyatt proposed to me yesterday, Maria." She blurted out the words that she hadn't even been able to share with Felicity.

Maria's eyebrows skyrocketed. She clasped her hands together over her heart. "Then why do you look so miserable?"

Because she was. "I turned him down."

Maria muttered a chanting "ay ay ay," as she pulled up the other chair and sat down. She folded her hands gently around Sarah-Jane's. "Do you love him?"

Sarah-Jane nodded.

"Then it will work out, niña."

"Wyatt doesn't forgive mistakes easily, Maria."

"Ah." She dismissed that with a shake of her head. "He's a man. Sometimes they don't learn as quickly as we women." She squeezed Sarah-Jane's hands. Where they weren't callused from knitting needles, they were soft. "I've been married to my Jose a very long time. Believe me. I know."

"You and Jose are perfect for each other."

"We are," Maria agreed. "But there have been many days when we most certainly don't feel like remembering that." Her eyes sparkled. "And then we do. And we go on. You always go on for someone you love. Even when you may, momentarily, want to strangle them." She leaned forward and lowered her voice to a whisper. "Why do you think I learned to knit so long ago? I could pretend I was jabbing him with the needle and not the yarn." She sat up again, nodding with satisfaction when Sarah-Jane smiled. "There. That's the smile I know."

Sarah-Jane didn't believe Maria's story about the knitting needles, but she didn't have to. "Oh, Maria." She exhaled. "I can't imagine what my life would be like if I hadn't met you. I love you."

Maria smiled. Patted her cheek. "And I love you, too, niña." Then she hopped up from her chair, much too spry to be the age she really was. "But *go*." She shooed her again with her hands. "Sit in the park. You'll feel better after some fresh air and sun."

So Sarah-Jane went. She didn't have a lunch with her because she hadn't felt like packing one. Hadn't felt like eating. She stopped at a drugstore along the way and bought a bottled water and a snack-size package of sunflower seeds in the shells. The birds, she knew, always felt like eating.

She crossed the street and entered the park. She told herself to pick a different bench. To sit by the lake. The birds ate sunflower seeds there just as well. Or by the playground equipment. She even headed that way, but as soon as she heard the giddy, childish screams of the little ones playing there, she thought of Wyatt's expression the day before. *You want children?*

She'd almost told him that she wanted his children.

She aimed away from the playground equipment.

Headed for her usual bench.

Silly to think that she'd be able to stay away. Like driving by a car accident and thinking that you won't even take a single, morbid glance. If the same old man with the cane was there, she'd sit there with him. Offer him a few seeds to throw at the birds. It would be better than shaking his cane at them, at least.

The bench *was* occupied.

But not by the old man.

The soles of her tennis shoes dragged, slowed against the path. Her chest went tight.

This man was young. And stubborn. With dark gold hair that fell across his forehead and brilliant blue eyes that could see right to the heart of her.

"Wyatt."

He'd stood the second she spotted him, and he flicked his hand at the bench. "I was afraid you wouldn't come."

Her eyes burned. "Did Maria know you were here?"

The quick tug of his eyebrows over his nose told her he didn't know what she was talking about. "No. Why?"

She shook her head. "It doesn't matter." She just sometimes had to wonder if Maria had acquired a magician's skills at some point in her life.

"Will you sit down?"

It was so clear on his face that he wasn't certain that she would. And it was unnerving to see him unnerved.

She moved to the bench on wobbly knees and sat. Propped the water bottle on the wood beside her and tore open the bag of seeds, taking care that her shaking fingers didn't make a mess of it. She pinched some seeds out of the opening and tossed them off to the side. A half dozen birds swooped.

They, at least, were comfortingly predictable.

"Why are you here, Wyatt?"

He didn't sit down beside her. Just stood there with his hands fisted in the pockets of his faded blue jeans, the soft brown Henley shirt he wore straining across his bunched shoulders. "I brought you lunch." He nodded toward the neatly folded brown paper sack that was next to her water bottle.

"I'm not really hungry," she murmured. "But thank you for the thought."

He looked oddly frustrated. But then he glanced away and she decided she must have imagined it. "How's Felicity?"

She rolled a seed back and forth between her fingers. "She's fine. Why?"

"Just asking," he murmured. Then he pulled one of his hands free and raked it through his hair. "And...you? Are you okay?"

She was dying inside. "Just peachy." She flipped the seed into the grass and pinched out a few more.

"You were right," he said abruptly.

Not from any angle that she could discern. From the moment she'd lied about her own name to him until she'd stood out on that beautiful piece of land with him, she'd done everything all wrong.

"When we first met," he continued doggedly when she remained silent, "you were a perfect distraction from everything I didn't want to think about."

She stared blindly at the cheerful red bag in her hands. She'd known it. But hearing him admit it was like having her skin peeled back.

"It took me a while to face the fact that the reason you were such an effective distraction was because I'd fallen in love with you."

Her fingers tightened and seeds squeezed out the top of the bag. She looked at up him. "I fell in love with you, too, Wyatt," she whispered. How easily she'd fallen.

He suddenly sat on the bench next to her, angled so he was facing her.

A few more seeds squeezed out. She absently brushed all of them off her jeans onto the grass.

"I meant what I said, Sarah-Jane. I want to marry you."

That muscle in his jaw worked a few times. "I want to have children with you. Grandchildren."

Her mouth went dry. She didn't bother reaching for the water bottle. The only thing that would quench this particular thirst was him.

She went still when his hand moved, thinking that he was going to reach for her, but all he did was pick up the brown-bag lunch he'd brought. Then he set it down again to rub his hand down his thigh. His eyes bored into hers. "I can give you as much time as you need to make up your mind whether you're willing to take me on, as long as I know you're going to be with me. Reminding me every time I forget to look for all the shades that exist between black and white. Reminding me that it's not just the end result that matters, but the journey in between."

She inhaled and her breath felt jagged.

"I know," he murmured. "Strange hearing that from me."

"Everything's feeling a little strange."

That muscle worked again. "Strange bad or strange good?"

She pressed her lips together for a moment. "Good."

He closed his eyes and exhaled. When he opened them again, she realized with shock that they were damp. "Knowing you as I do, however—" his voice was husky "—I know that just saying something doesn't necessarily convince you of it. You seem to generally need...proof. Proof I've definitely been more than willing to provide."

Her body flushed.

"So," he continued slowly, softly, "it dawned on me that if I gave you proof that I mean what I say about our future, maybe you'd let me rewind the last few weeks of mistakes I've made, and give *me* a fresh start. This is new for me. But I promise you I'll improve. And I'll never leave you again."

She'd give him anything as long as he didn't stop loving her. "Wyatt—"

He lifted the brown bag again. "Will you have lunch with me, Sarah-Jane?"

She let out a choked laugh. Blinked at the tears blinding her and took the bag. She opened it, pulled out the paper-wrapped sandwich. As soon as she unwrapped it, another choking laugh caught in her throat. "Peanut butter and jelly."

"If you're going to indulge, do it right," he murmured.

She pressed her hand to her lips, not really caring that tears were sliding down her face and her nose had turned all stuffy and was probably red to boot. "I shouldn't have told you no yesterday, Wyatt. I—"

"You told me exactly what we both needed." He pushed off the bench and stood in front of her. He shoved his fists back into his pockets and rocked back and forth on the heels of his battered cowboy boots a few times.

It was wholly bemusing to see him so nervous. "I flew to Atlanta yesterday afternoon," he finally said.

Her lips parted. The proof, she realized. The proof he'd said she wanted. "You saw your father?"

"In the flesh." His jaw flexed. "First time in over a month." He exhaled. Paced a few steps one direction, then the other. "He looked like hell. And he still didn't offer any explanation about what he's done. But we talked."

"Was there anything left to talk about?"

"Plenty, as it happens." He stopped once more, right in front of her. "Red Rock, for one. He knows I'm not going back to Atlanta. But now he knows my not going back isn't for the same reason it once was." He suddenly gestured toward the paper bag. "There's more in there."

She hadn't taken a single bite of the sandwich. The last thing she cared about was food, when every word out of his mouth was making hope take wing inside her. But to satisfy him, she reached back into the bag, felt the square at the bottom, and pulled it out. Only when his gaze flicked away from hers toward her hand did she glance down.

It was a silk-covered ring box.

And her eyes suddenly swam all over again.

Wyatt went down on one knee, scattering the birds that had decided to avail themselves of the sunflower seeds spilling out of her forgotten bag, and took the box from her. He opened it up and pulled out a diamond ring that flashed white fire in the sun. "It wasn't very long ago that I told my brothers that I'd never be interested in doing the bended knee thing."

His voice turned gruff and when he took her hand, he was no more steady than she. "And then I danced with you on a bridge in San Antonio. And I sat on this park bench and watched you feed your birds. And the only thing I'm finding myself interested in is kneeling here with you until you promise to give me another chance. The reason why I want to make Red Rock my home is because it is your home. I want to give you everything, Sarah-Jane, because you are everything I need. Will you be my wife?"

She exhaled shakily. Her heart hadn't turned to shards. How could it when it was overflowing? "I don't want you kneeling at my feet like the prince in some fairy-tale fantasy," she said huskily. She leaned toward him, laying her hand along the muscle working in his jaw. "Real life is so much better and I want you beside me. Whether we're making love or whether we're arguing. I want you beside me when we're laughing," she brushed her thumb over the single, damp trail at the corner of his beautiful, beautiful blue eyes, "or we're crying. I want to have your babies. And spoil your grandchildren. I want everything, Wyatt. And I want it only with you." She stood, tugging on him to stand as well, and the peanut butter sandwich fell to the ground. The rest of the sunflower seeds scattered.

Birds flocked down around them, filling the air with the sounds of their frenzied excitement.

"We're going to have to put a few bird feeders outside our bedroom window, aren't we?" he murmured.

She smiled slowly and reached up to press her lips against his. "Yes," she whispered. "I'll be your wife."

He covered her lips with his. Then he threw his head back and laughed, and lifted her around the waist and swung her in a circle, causing the birds to take wing as one.

"And, yes," she laughed with him, loving him so much she was flying higher than any bird ever could. And he was right there with her. Where he always would be. "We are going to need several bird feeders."

* * * *

*Don't miss the next chapter
in the new Special Edition continuity*
THE FORTUNES OF TEXAS: SOUTHERN INVASION

Single-minded Michael Fortune comes to Red Rock to talk sense into his crazy cousins—and avoid an irreparable family feud. Romance was not in his plans...until he falls for innocent businesswoman Felicity Thomas! Could an affair with this polar opposite keep this Fortune in Texas— for keeps?

*Look for A DATE WITH FORTUNE
by Susan Crosby
On sale February 2013,
wherever Harlequin Books are sold.*

REQUEST YOUR FREE BOOKS!

2 FREE NOVELS PLUS 2 FREE GIFTS!

Wild for the Sheriff

by Kathleen O'Brien

On sale February 5

Dallas Garwood had always known that sooner or later he'd
open a door, turn a corner or look up from his desk and see
Rowena Wright standing there.

It wasn't logical. It was simply an unshakable certainty that
she wasn't gone for good, that one day she would return.

Not to see him, of course. He didn't kid himself that their
brief interlude had been important to her. But she'd be back
for Bell River—the ranch that was part of her.

Still, he hadn't thought today would be the day he'd face her
across the threshold of her former home.

Or that she would look so gaunt. Her beauty was still there,
but buried beneath some kind of haggard exhaustion. Her
wild green eyes were circled with shadows, and her white shirt
and jeans hung on her.